THE
LIKES OF ME

Also by Randall Beth Platt

Out of a Forest Clearing
The Four Arrows Fe-As-Ko
The Royalscope Fe-As-Ko
The Cornerstone

For Young Readers

Honor Bright

THE
LIKES OF ME

RANDALL BETH PLATT

Delacorte Press

Published by
Delacorte Press
an imprint of
Random House Children's Books
a division of Random House, Inc.
1540 Broadway
New York, New York 10036

Library of Congress Cataloging-in-Publication Data

Platt, Randall Beth.
    The likes of me / Randall Beth Platt.
        p.   cm.
    Summary: In 1918, having run away from the Washington State lumber camp she calls home, a fourteen-year-old half-Chinese albino named Cordy makes her way to Seattle and finds work in a carnival.
    ISBN 0-385-32692-0
    [1. Runaways Fiction.   2. Carnivals Fiction.   3. Albinos and albinism Fiction. 4. Chinese Americans Fiction.   5. Racially mixed people Fiction.   6. Washington (State) Fiction.]   I. Title.
PZ7.P7120Li   2000
[Fic]—dc21   99-33284
                                                                  CIP

The text of this book is set in 13-point Centaur.
Book design by Patrice Sheridan
Manufactured in the United States of America

February 2000

10   9   8   7   6   5   4   3   2   1

BVG

To
Lance and Kristi,
whom I love a lot

1

They called her Babe. But not because she was beautiful. Far from it. And it wasn't because she was sweet or innocent or childlike. They called her Babe because she was as strong as an ox—Paul Bunyan's blue ox, to be exact. Since she could beat any man to a pulp in the small lumber camp of Centner's Mill, folks smiled respectful-like when they called her Babe. They gave her a wide berth, too, not because her gigantic frame required it, but because no one wanted to risk crossing Babe. And Lord help the soul who said she was hardy breeding stock.

There's a kind of self-confidence, maybe even arrogance, that comes when you're big. You can hide all sorts of things—even your age. Babe was the kind of woman who hid her age well. She could have been twenty-five. She could have been forty-five. No one had the courage to ask. And it hardly mattered. Nearly six-feet-ten and over three hundred fifty pounds, she could be as old or as young as she wanted to be. She had arms like forged steel and a face of serene strength

that comes when you know no one is going to bother you—
ever. Babe could have told the men of the camp she was the
Queen of Egypt and not one man would have broken a
smile. More likely they'd bow, ask after Marc Anthony and
get out of her way.

Her real name was Fern Killingsworth. She arrived one fall
day in 1911 at the West Coast Lumber Company, Western
Washington Division, Centner's Mill office, to apply for a
job. My father was superintendent of all operations. I was
seven years old and playing in my father's office. Since my
mother had died that summer, my father had to drag me to
work every day. Even at seven, I knew I was a bother to him.
Even at seven, I knew my life was about to change when the
door flew open, bringing in a chilly breeze and a rustling of
dead leaves. I looked up from the floor under my father's
huge desk, where I'd fashioned a small neighborhood for my
dolls.

My father didn't look up. He couldn't have or else he
wouldn't have barked, "Close the door, damn it! There goes
all the heat!"

I'd never seen such a large person. The entire doorjamb
was filled with this stranger, wrapped in a huge overcoat,
with a muffler that must have been a mile long going from
around the shoulders, up and around the head to anchor a
large felt hat, back around the neck and then down to the
knees, where it swayed in the breeze.

The door closed and my father finally looked up. I inched
back closer to his chair and clutched my favorite doll to my
chest, as though we were going to need each other's protec-
tion.

The gloved hands unwrapped the muffler, and slowly we
watched the giant before us emerge. The gloves came off

next—the hands were large, white and even sort of elegant. Then the hat—the hair was thick and plaited into neat, organized spirals. Then the coat. The giant's body was thick and sturdy like a cedar. Not fat, not unfit, but strong and reliable.

I inched even farther back. The giant spoke. She offered her hand to my father. "I come about the job. Name's Fern Killingsworth. Folks call me Babe and I come about the job." Her voice was deep, growly, mannish.

I couldn't see my father's face, but I could tell by his voice that he was awestruck—just like me and my dolls. "Which job?" he asked. That still makes me laugh. My father was hardly ever confused, or if he was, no one knew it but him. There were no other women in the camp and only two jobs posted: Cook team and mule skinner. I guess my father thought he'd found his mule skinner.

Instead of answering, the giant put the ad from the *Aberdeen Daily World* down on his desk and pointed to the words "cook team."

"Miss Killingsworth, come spring we sign on a hundred men, maybe more. That's why we're looking for a cook team. Too much work for just one woman. The ad asks for a couple. You know, a man and his wife."

"I'll work harder'n three men and their wives," she answered. I dared a peek from behind my father's chair. She was staring straight down at me and I ducked back fast, hitting my head on the drawer. I knew I looked as strange to her as she did to me.

My father stood up. He was far from the tallest or strongest man in the camp. Babe towered over him. Then he said what must have been a very brave thing. He said, "We had a single woman here cooking once and it didn't work out. Too many men away from the city too long. If you know what I mean."

Again I peeked up. She had a wide face with cheekbones like ledges, huge black eyes, a straight, gallant nose and large, square front teeth framed by full lips. Everything about her was larger than life. I couldn't take my eyes off her as she spoke down to my father.

"You really think men bother . . . me?" She stepped back to let her size sink in. Then she added without the trace of a smile, "If *you* know what *I* mean."

My father waited before replying. She could probably do the work of six men, but I was crossing my fingers he would make her leave. You see, I was hoping our new cook would be more like my mother, whom I missed like anything. I was praying for a warm, kind, small Chinese woman. Someone who could sing me to sleep, laugh me awake, teach me the things I wanted to know, and who would make my father's meanness go away. I wanted my mother back. Not this giant intruder taking up half the office. I tugged on my father's pant leg and whispered, "Father . . ."

He ignored me and I ignored him ignoring me and said louder, "Father . . ."

"Cordelia, I told you, you can only play here if you let me do my work," he said, shaking my small grip off his pant leg.

It was hardly the attention I was looking for. I looked up at the giant, terrified.

"You keep your child under your desk?" she asked. "Not at school?"

My father always stiffened up when someone questioned him about me, especially since my mother had died. But before he could speak, she added, "I read, write, cipher some. Speak some German, some French. Chinook Jargon too."

"I don't need a scholar. I need a cook," he said, probably wondering how he was going to get this person out of his office without wrecking anything.

It was then the alarm in the mill went off.

It's funny how some things you immediately just know. The alarm was the same one that sounded every morning, every noon and every evening, bringing the workers to the mill or telling them when to eat or when to quit. But, like we all had a clock inside our heads, everyone in Centner's Mill knew it wasn't any of those times. Somehow the horn blasted more loudly, more urgently, when it did for an emergency—that first long blast, followed by six shorter ones.

I froze. The last time the alarm had wailed like that was when my mother had fallen into the river early that summer. She'd gotten herself all tangled in her long skirts; the current had pulled her under a jam of logs, and she'd drowned.

My father was out of the office like lightning. I wondered if he was remembering that horrible June day like I was. The woman followed him. I didn't know why. Maybe it was something all folks who'd spent time in a lumber mill just automatically did. I was alone in the office. I grabbed up my favorite doll, Gert, and went to the window. I know I was shaking because I remember telling Gert to quit shaking, that everything was going to be okay, there was nothing to be scared of. The alarm goes off all the time, I told her, even for slivers, bee stings, little cuts and such.

I watched my father run into the mill, followed by the giant stranger. My breath fogged the window. Dogs barked over the shouting and finally someone turned the alarm off and it was suddenly deathly quiet. The door to the office flew open with a gust of wind, as though granting me permission to run to the mill and see for myself what had gone wrong.

The large metal doors were wide open by the time I got there. I was so small that it was easy for me to weave my way through the men standing about. I can still feel Gert close against my chest as I walked. Why I brought her, I don't know.

I heard a scream. I don't think I'd ever heard a real scream before. Crying, even wailing, but never an all-out scream. This was a man's scream. Monty McGuire's scream. All I could see was half of him. I crept closer. Some peeler logs must have jammed on the conveyor overhead and, before anyone could pull the emergency switch, a load had fallen onto Monty. Two men were holding on to his arms, maybe to pull him out, and he was screaming for them not to. Then others were starting to pull the smaller logs off—three and four men to a log. My father was shouting orders to pull a block and tackle rigging over, throw chains around those logs, you here, you there!

Poor Monty. He was screaming that he couldn't feel his legs. Then, in all the confusion, the strange giant woman walked out of the crowd. She stood watching the men struggling with the logs that pinned Monty down. As they teamed and counted "One, two, three—lift," as they grunted, and as the wind blew through the mill, the giant walked closer to the heap. I'll never know if it was her calm expression in that horrible moment or whether it was her size that made the men stop and look up. She seemed to be studying the pile of logs, like they were just a giant's game of pickup sticks. Then she pointed for two men to take that end, two to take the other end of the top log. They protested, said that that might make the rest of the pile crash down on Monty. She said no. She *knew*. Then she said, "You three—when I say 'Clear,' pull him out. Then you four men, take that log and jam it in when he's clear."

My father tried pulling her back, but it was like she never felt him on her arm. She approached the log on Monty's legs, lay down next to it, pulled her skirts up to free her legs and put her huge feet under the crushing log. First her face blushed, then it turned bright red as she pressed her legs up under the log. Slowly, slowly it started to rise. She herself screamed as though that brought her strength. Then she fell silent, took a deep breath, and closed her eyes so tight that tears squeezed out. And then with a sound that echoed through the mill and will echo in me forever, she screamed, "Clear!"

In one swift move, Monty was pulled free and the other log was jammed in while she held that crushing log up with the strength of her two legs. When the new log was shoved in Monty's place, to keep the whole pile steady, she bent her knees and brought the log down slowly, carefully, until it rested on the pile. Then she rolled almost gracefully to her side and stood up. Like it had all been a circus act, only the strong man was named Fern Killingsworth, known as Babe.

She dusted herself off, adjusted her skirt, and then looked at my father, who stood as speechless as the rest of us.

"I am also strong," she stated.

"Come to the office and we'll fill out the papers," my father replied, smiling for the first time, I think, since my mother had died four months earlier. He arranged for the crushed man's aid, then led the way out of the mill.

Monty McGuire was one of my favorites and I quickly ran over to him as they loaded him on the first-aid board.

"You okay, Monty?" I asked, taking his cold, shaking hand.

"Who was that woman?" he asked weakly.

"She's come to cook. Can't you walk?"

"Sure I can. I'm just tired. You run off after your daddy, Cordy."

They put a blanket over him, but he was still shaking. The usually sweet smell from the shavings in the mill was now mixed with the smell of sweat and fear. Maybe I was smelling blood, I don't know. He was bleeding badly, for I saw the blood soak into the gray wool blanket.

They had brought a truck around and quickly loaded him in. I watched them take him away. He never came back. No use for halfies in a lumber camp. Harry, the mill foreman, noticed I was standing alone with only my doll for comfort. The giant and my father had disappeared into his office and I was still shaking. Harry picked me up and told me my doll was looking a little blue and wasn't I foolish for bringing her outside without her coat? I nodded yes and he carried us both back toward the office.

"Never seen anything like it in my whole entire life," he said. I knew what he was talking about. "That woman. Strong as a ox, she is."

"That's her name," I informed him importantly. "Her name is Babe."

"Well then, I'd say she's got herself a fittin' name. Yessir, a real fittin' name."

2

My name is Cordelia Lu Hankins. I was born on December 28, 1903, a Capricorn in the Year of the Rabbit. My mother was Chinese, brought over by her family and sold as an indentured laundry girl. Indentured was the nice way of saying enslaved. Your family gets the money and you get the work until you've worked off your indenture price. Or until someone buys it. Which was what my father did in order to marry her. It wasn't until she died that it occurred to me he really loved her. Or maybe it was a case of "you don't know what you've got till it's gone." My father never showed her much affection. He treated my mother coolly. In fact, I always thought that's what it meant when a Chinese person was called a coolie—that's how you treated them. But my mother accepted this—as though she knew "her place." You couldn't forget "your place" with my father to remind you. His word was never challenged, including his orders that my mother never speak in Chinese to me, never dress me in silk pajamas or even tell me about my Oriental heritage.

Of course, she spoke some English . . . just the basics. My father spoke some Chinese . . . also just the basics. My father did a lot of my mother's talking for her. Makes me wonder how much got lost in the translation.

But what my mother and I couldn't say right out to each other, we communicated in other ways . . . a look, a touch, a smile. She was my very existence—until that summer when I was seven. Then she was gone and it was just my father and me.

My father, William "Red" Hankins, was Caucasian, and as you might have guessed by his nickname, he had red hair. I used to wonder if it was because my mother was yellow with black hair, and my father was white with red hair, that I came out albino—without any color at all, as though all the color in my family had been used up. My hair is white and much of my face looks Oriental. Except my eyes are . . . well, they look pink but that's because they have no color. And my eyes don't hold still—they are always darting back and forth. They call it nystagmus, but having a medical word for it didn't make it easier on anybody. My vision doesn't move, but my eyes do. My vision isn't the greatest, but I can see all I have ever needed to. I've been called Pinkie, Chinkie, Whitey, Bunny, Rare Bit, and Pale Face. But my name is Cordelia. Most folks just call me Cordy.

My father had worked hard to get where he was. How many times had I heard him say that? He did a job, collected his pay, like any other workingman.

I don't know much about my father's beginnings. If he had family somewhere, he never talked about them. Of course, you have to understand the makings of a lumberjack, which is how my father started out. These aren't men who like walking on concrete. Take what you probably know about cowboys, only substitute trees for cows, take away the friendship with a horse and put in the wail of a steam donkey, and that's more like a lumberjack. Then multiply the injuries, dismemberments and deaths. . . . No, I don't think you become a lumberjack if you need friends. The only long relationship there could ever be in the forest was with a tree and even that was doomed, eventually.

So, when my father left the city for the woods, it was a decision for his lifetime. And he was deciding *my* lifetime, too. Having the burden of me only placed us deeper into the forest.

I know this because I remember my father talking to someone on the phone once. It was one of those long-distance phone calls where the operator lets you know when and where to be and then she connects the lines. A long-distance phone call in Centner's Mill was always a special occasion. So I knew it had to be from distant lands. Maybe even Chicago. Naturally I stayed close to the office that day, excited to even imagine that someone, maybe even thousands of miles away, was talking to my father. The call came through and I could tell by the way my father was talking, he wasn't going to take me anywhere, ever. It sounded like he was being offered something really big. I'll never forget him looking at *me* while he talked. By that time, I was doing clerk work in the mill office. I pretended to be busy filing, but I could see him in the reflection of the picture of Abraham Lincoln above the cabinet. He looked right at my back and said into the phone, "Well, I appreciate you thinking of me, Mr. Steele, but we're happy right here at the mill."

He said "we're." Not "I'm." Of course, he was thinking about me . . . his little white thorn. I knew from the day my mother died how my father truly felt about me. He was a dedicated man, I suppose maybe even a decent man, but not a family man. He wasn't meant to be the father and sole parent to a girl the likes of me. A man like my father needed sons he could send into the woods, slap on their backs as they came back with skidders of logs, say "Well, done, boys!" and compare to other men's sons. Instead, he had me.

In June 1913, when I was nine, we moved into a larger home my father had built in a grove of trees just outside Centner's Mill. When I asked him why we needed a bigger home, since it was just the two of us, he looked at me and announced, "Babe is moving in."

I should have guessed it from the first moment my father let me walk into our new home. The ceilings were high, but what should have tipped me off were the doorjambs—seven feet high, they were. And the kitchen. Why were the counters built so high? They came almost to my forehead. Either he was expecting me to grow a few feet that summer or else . . . Oh yes, I should have seen that Babe was coming.

In the two years Babe had been our camp cook we had had our ups and downs, except Babe had all the ups and I had all the downs. I knew, if she wanted to, she could kill me by sitting on me, or maybe with just her wicked glance. Every time I looked at Babe I felt one of two things: sheer terror or absolute awe. No one ever accused her of being maternal or affectionate or even kind, especially when she was, as my father would call it, "on a toot." On a toot meant drinking. She didn't do it often, but when she did . . . look out, Centner's Mill. Look out, Cordy.

So, when my father told me Babe was moving in, I asked, "What for?"

"It's too inconvenient going back and forth to the cook-house for our meals. The new place is just too far away.

Besides, you're growing up and need the advice and comfort of a woman. And Babe says her rheumatism has been acting up in her cabin, what with just that old woodstove. It's agreed all around."

Well, I hadn't agreed. "I don't like Babe and I don't want her around," I said boldly.

My father looked at me and replied, "I'm doing this for you, you know."

"Doing what?"

"Marrying Babe."

That's when the floor dropped out from under me. I didn't say a thing. Just went to my room and closed the door. I crawled into bed, clutching a photo of my mother, and cried. I thought about poor Cinderella and her wicked stepmother. Now I was about to get my very own.

What I remember most vividly about that summer was me, nine years old, looking up into the face of Babe when she and my father had come back from the justice of the peace. Married.

"I ain't calling you Mother," I said.

"Good. 'Cause I ain't your mother," she said down to me.

"Ain't calling you nothing."

"Suits me. But when your belly's aching or when your clothes don't fit you'll sure call me something. And that something better be Babe and it better be with a smile."

That pretty much set the tone for our relationship. I tried not to tremble when she entered a room, I tried to look straight up into her face, but the fact of the matter was, Babe just scared the boots off of me.

Of course, I wasn't the only one Babe scared the boots off of. It was just after they got married. I was whacking the rugs on the outside line. I was hopeless at it, but when Babe did it she whacked so hard that she'd either bend the beater, break it altogether or sometimes snap the clothesline clean off the pole. So it was my job to beat the rugs. I hated it. I'd work up a sweat, and no matter which direction the wind was blowing I was always downwind of it. Then my sweaty face would get all the dust I'd just whacked out of the rug. I looked even scarier than usual when I finished.

A kitchenware salesman had driven into the mill yard to sell my father something that day. Well, his rig was shiny new and painted bright red and you know how rare red carriages are. He had a wonderful white horse and I just couldn't resist a closer look.

So there I was, looking like a moon-maiden, my face covered in dust, my hair undone and wild, sneaking toward the offices for a closer look. The horse was tied up at the front gate and he must have sensed something strange was approaching. Horses always seem to know when I'm around. The horse turned and saw me, and it got a little nervous. Of course, I loved horses and didn't get a chance to get this close to one very often. What I didn't realize was that Babe was following me, no doubt wondering where her rug whacker was running off to.

The horse began to startle, no matter how beautiful I said he was or how much fresh grass I held out or how gingerly I approached. The salesman was coming out of the office with a sample crate of the dinnerware he was peddling. Well, somewhere between my tripping over my skirts, the salesman yelling at me and then dropping the crate of dishes, and Babe running toward us like a stampeding buffalo, the horse broke loose—just snapped his reins and ran off down the road.

The peddler started yelling at me.

"Get away from that horse, you little freak! Don't you know something like you . . ."

The peddler bent over to pick up his dishes, swearing a blue streak at me and making me cry. I watched the horse and the red carriage disappear down the road. My father was probably going to hear about this.

Suddenly a big shadow came over the peddler. He paused, looked up and saw Babe.

"You call this girl a little freak?" she growled.

The man slowly rose and said, "Oh my God . . ."

"You got a horse to catch," she said, stepping between me and the broken dishes.

He backed away, his face about as terrified as any I had ever seen. He started to run after his horse and you should have seen how good a thrower Babe was. She started hurling those dishes after the peddler man and hit her moving target three times.

I just stood there, with my mouth wide open and my tears vanished.

When she'd hurled the last plate, she looked down at me and said, "What you gawkin' at, girl? You git back to them rugs and you git back now!"

I ran back to the rugs and didn't stop beating them until the last speck of dust was floating out over Centner's Mill.

In 1918, my father built a still larger home—not more rooms, just a more important house to "fit Babe," he said. It was as though, as the mill grew, as the town grew, so did my father's status, and the superintendent's home had to be— well, "fittin'."

This one he built up on a hill overlooking the cove in the

millpond. My room had a wonderful view of the pond, the hills beyond, the western sky. And since I was now fourteen, I seemed to spend more time in my room and I couldn't have been happier with it. You see, up until I was fourteen, I was merely curious to look at. Then things began to change in all directions of my life. I became possibly the ugliest thing you've ever seen and hiding away in my room seemed like a mercy for all concerned. In fact, by the time I turned fourteen, it became pretty obvious why my father had kept us hidden in the woods for all those years. It was to keep me away from the glaring, laughing eyes of the outside world. "You stay out of the sun, Cordelia," he used to say. "You keep yourself to the shady side of the street, you hear?" And I did.

So the summer of 1918 began for me in a new home, which I loved. I still avoided Babe like the Spanish influenza. My father's position that summer took on new importance as the mill started to grow and as new logging sections were opened.

The summer of 1918 was also the summer I met Squirl.

3

Squirl. Even saying his name cues a kiss. Squirl. So called for his amazing ability to leap around life and land safely, one-footed and balanced. You meet a person like Squirl maybe once in a lifetime, if you're lucky or if you're cursed. Squirl was daring, Squirl was confidence, Squirl was life.

Squirl worked the log booms. He was so graceful as he danced across the slippery logs in the pond and along the North River that fed it that the seasoned crew just stood on their logs and marveled. His corked boots barely seemed to touch the logs. Watch a squirrel run along the ground, up a tree, across a branch, laughing as it goes, and you'll understand. Squirl was a natural-born river rat.

We were having dinner when my father told Babe he'd just hired a new hand that day for the log rafts.

Babe looked at him with great suspicion. I knew what she was thinking. So did my father. He said, "He's only a boy, Babe. You know I don't hire me any draft dodgers in this outfit. Besides, a good boom man is hard to find, during wartime or any other."

"Bet he's runnin' away from something, then," Babe grumbled, heaping a mountain of mashed potatoes onto her plate, then passing the meager remains on to me.

"Naw, this boy's one of those free spirits—said so himself. Been on his own all his life."

"Great. All's we need around here's one more wandering soul," Babe said down to her plate. "Hmmmmph! Free spirit. Don't matter if they punch cattle or punch logs or punch time clocks at some big city factory, free spirits just wander from job to job, taking lots and leavin' nothin'! Don't need us any brush ape boomers in this camp!"

Then she aimed her fork at me and said, "And don't you go gettin' to likin' him, 'cause he'll be gone come winter. You stay away from the likes of him. No-good drifter, five'll get you ten."

My father must have agreed, for he forbade me to even talk to his new river hand. For a man who claimed to be an atheist, he sure used the words "evil" and "wrath" and "by God!" often enough. Babe just looked up from the bowl of gravy she was holding and looked square at me, then at my father, then back down to the gravy. As I was getting older, I was being cast "that look" more and more. No explanations, just "that look"—as though I had better keep my mouth shut, my eyes low and my opinions to myself.

So naturally, I was curious. So curious, in fact, that it was now an obligation that I get to know this Squirl. At the first opportunity I went down to the shore of the log pond. I wanted to see this water sprite—someone whom I was forbidden to talk to, to know, to even look at, must be someone worth knowing! I sat on the hillside and wrapped my skirts around me.

There were five or six men out on the logs that morning. I could recognize them by their colorful felt hats. I can't speak for other camps, but the loggers and mill workers in Centner's Mill took great pride in the hats they wore. No two were the same. My father said it really helped knowing who you were signaling to across the pond, across the mill or across a clearing. This was especially helpful to me—I'd learned early on to compensate for my poor eyesight by recognizing colors and movement. But there was someone out there on the boom who had no hat. He seemed to skip across the logs with the balance of a cat, chips of bark kicking up behind him. The other boom men would stand, hop, stop, balance themselves with their pike poles before stabbing and maneuvering a log. I'd watched them a million times. But this new boy would almost dance along—more performer than worker. Watching him I knew, I just knew, this was Squirl.

He fell into the water four times in the hour I sat watching. I could hear the men's laughter from clear up on the hillside. Each time, Squirl would pull himself back out of the water, laugh back at them, issue a challenge and move faster, work harder than before. My father knew what he was doing when he hired men—evil drifters or not.

I suppose, even from the distance where I first sat watching him, I fell in love with Squirl. From the echoes of his laughter off the log boom, I knew more life had just entered Centner's Mill than I had ever known.

Of course, I had to watch him from a distance. No doubt he'd never seen anything the likes of me. By fourteen, I was learning how to darken my skin with yesterday's coffee grounds, how to put up my hair and keep it well under my hat and wear smoked glasses everywhere, not only to shield my eyes from the brightness of day but to shield other people's eyes from the sight of mine. I knew I was a curiosity. And the changes that were starting in me didn't help. My nose looked bigger, a timid little chest was appearing and pimples the size of Mount Saint Helens broke out on my forehead. But when I questioned Babe about all these changes, she just turned and grunted, "Hmph! Git used to it! And it don't git no easier!"

So falling in love with Squirl from a distance was just fine with me. I was happy to watch him along the logs, or to follow him at a great distance and with a casual, just-on-my-way-to-town step. Best of all, I loved to sit and overhear stories the men in camp told about him. As I filed in the office or walked time cards to the mill or pulled laundry off the line for Babe, I listened. "Hal, did you hear what that Squirl did today?" or "By God, Hap, if I hadn't seen it with my own two eyes, I wouldn'ta believed it!" or "If that kid lives to see twenty, I'll be gull durned!" or "Whoever named him Squirl ain't never seen a monkey!" Hearing things like this made me somehow proud that I had chosen Squirl to love. Yes, proud. And yet, for the first month he'd been at the mill, I had avoided meeting him face-to-face. Not because of my father's warnings or Babe's looks, but because it was going to have to be perfect. I couldn't let it happen until everything was right. Either that, or maybe I was just plain scared to meet Squirl at all.

Perhaps he had even heard about me—that poor white thing, the boss man's daughter—that elephant for a step-mother, hidden away from the world. Poor little thing, Cordelia. I was sure this was the way the men of Centner's Mill—and their wives—referred to me. Since I seldom mingled in town, since I was schooled at home, since I didn't go to church, I only had my own little imagination to rely on. But people talk. If you're different, then you know—those hushed conversations as you pass, those patronizing smiles, those welts on your back from their stares of pity after you walk by.

But no matter how much you plan, things are going to just happen anyway. Like on that Wednesday. On Wednesdays I filed, ran errands, answered the phone for my father while he did business down in Aberdeen. Now that I was older, he gave me the job of holding down the fort.

The bell over the door rang. I looked up and it was Squirl. One hand was wrapped in his shirt, and his bare chest was glistening wet through his suspenders. On one of his famous spills, he must have cut his hand. He held it out to me as though I was going to be the judge of whether or not he would have to go to the doctor or back to work.

"They sent me up here, ma'am," he said, catching blood as it dripped off his elbow. Ma'am? I thought. Then I remembered that, from across the room, with my white hair sticking out from under my cap and my dowdy-fit clothes, he probably thought he was talking to the camp matron—someone's little old grandmother. So I stayed across the room, close to the file cabinets. My heart was leaping against my chest. Thank God I'd turned down the gas lamps, so the light didn't shine off my skin and blind him. I knew I had to say something, but I seemed to be stuck to the floor and held captive by the file cabinet.

"Hell, it's just a scratch," he said, probably thinking I was going to faint at the sight of blood. "You the nurse?"

I closed the drawer, walked to my father's desk, pulled out a sheet of paper and said, "No, just a clerk."

He looked around the room, then said, "Sign on the door said First Aid."

"Oh. That's because I have to fill out this voucher. Then I'll send you to the doctor in town."

"Ever have someone bleed to death while you fill out your voucher?" he asked. I couldn't look him in the eyes, so I didn't know if he was joking or angry or bleeding to death.

I had him show me the wound and I tried to look calm and professional. After all, I'd seen fingers dangling by a shred before, but his thumb was more on than off.

By fourteen, I had learned how to keep my eyes well away from other people's eyes. Babe called it ostriching—thinking that if I didn't look at them, they couldn't see me. Said it worked for her, although I thought if you were even in the same *county* you could still see Babe. But I could almost feel Squirl's eyes investigating me no matter how much I didn't look at him. I prayed to God for the phone to ring, for the emergency alarm to blast, for the sky to explode, for the sun to sink. Anything, just let this moment of agony be over.

Finally, I couldn't stand it any longer. I looked up at him. He smiled and said, "You ain't old at all. Why, you're just a kid. What'd you do," he continued, touching a frizz of my hair from under my cap, "fall into your mama's bleach tank?"

I quickly tucked the escaping hair back under my cap and asked, "Full name?"

"Squirl. Just put down Squirl. That's how I'm known everywhere. Los Angeles, Frisco, Portland, Seattle. Just put down Squirl. 'S-Q-U-I-R-L.' "

"But . . ."

Then he flashed his time card in front of my face and

that's all it said. If my father had agreed to do that, then just Squirl it was.

"How can you see to write in here? Ain't it awful dark? Don't you folks pay your light bill?" he asked.

I knew he was looking at my eyes. It was the one thing no one could take their own steady-normal eyes off of.

"Don't that twitch drive you crazy?" he asked.

"I can see just fine, thank you." I ripped the voucher off the pad, gave it to him and told him where Doc Hathaway's office was.

My heart was still pounding. If I got him out of the office fast enough, I thought, maybe I wouldn't faint. Yet the last thing in the world I wanted was for him to leave. Now that I had him up close, I just wanted to look at him. God, if only I could be invisible. How many times in my life had I prayed for that?

He took the voucher, rewrapped his hand and said thanks. Then he asked me when he could go back to the "boomin' grounds."

"Doc Hathaway says," I replied, feeling a little more relaxed now that he was inching away.

"What if he says a week?"

"Then you can't work out there for a week."

"And what am I supposed to do for a week, knit socks for the Red Cross?"

I could think of a million things, but I said, as my father had trained me, "Report to the mill. They'll find you something until the doc says you can go back out on the logs."

"You mean *me* be a bullcook or flunky? *Me?* Ain't that a waste of my God-given talents?"

"Company rules," I replied.

He ran his good hand through his long hair to paste it

back, then he left. Once he was gone, I sat down, memorizing everything about him. His tan face and bright brown eyes and dark hair falling into them. How his whole face came alive when he spoke and how his jaw sort of cocked to the side, smiling, when he suggested I had fallen into the washtub. I had never, ever seen teeth so white or a smile as handsome as Squirl's. And Squirl hadn't stopped smiling from the moment he'd stepped in—including while he watched me look at his cut hand. This I know, because Squirl had a smile you could *feel*. I felt it on my hair, on my face, on my hands, on my eyes.

And, in the wonder of Squirl up close, in the warmth of his smile, came the instant realization of why my father had forbidden me to go near him. Squirl was, like me, also a half-breed. Only his other half was most definitely Indian.

We got the *Aberdeen Daily World* on the evening supply train
and I'd always have to wait for my father to finish reading it.
Then I'd take the paper from the kindling box, steal away to
my room and read it cover to cover. Even the ads. The war in
Europe, of course, took up most of the headlines, but the
worldwide influenza epidemic was taking up more and more
space. Of course, from atop our mountain, I didn't actually
know anyone who'd gone to war or who had survived or even
died from the flu, but it made for great reading. The paper
had a daily war column with the names of those enlisted,
those killed, those missing, those returning. It also had a
"sick" column with the names of those stricken, those recov-
ering and those who'd lost the battle. The obituaries made
for the best reading.

Then there was the latest news of the lumber mill strikes.
Now, I didn't ever know the exact details, because these were
the articles my father had cut out of the paper. I wondered if

he was keeping a scrapbook or if he just didn't want me or Babe to know how bad things were getting in our industry.

Although our mill was not yet affected, there were rumblings as the word of the larger mills striking started to creep up the West Coast from Coos Bay to Astoria on into Washington—Longview, Aberdeen, us. My father didn't say much and it was Babe who told me, "It'll come. Strikes always come. Well, strikes be damned. I've swung me a ax before. It's easy as pie. I did it before and I can do it again. In for a dime, in for a dollar, I always say."

Sitting there in that special, king-size chair my father had built for her, at the head of our dining room table, she looked every bit the giant I had first seen years ago when I was only seven. No matter how much I grew, it seemed she grew just as much. More. I never got used to her size. She still scared me when she entered a room, especially our mill offices, where she had to duck under the lintel. But she sort of smiled when she spoke that morning and I had no doubt in my mind that Babe could swing an ax and probably the fallen tree, too.

"But do you think our mill would strike, Babe?" I asked. "All those men turn on Father?"

Babe looked at me, put down her coffee cup, so small, so fragile in her hand, and said, "You get a few of those Wobbly union men stirrin' things up and our mill will strike in a heartbeat. Loyalty don't have nothin' to do with higher wages and shorter hours. Fact is, loyalty don't have nothin' to do with nothin'."

Any chance I saw to sneak into Babe's past I took, for she seldom spoke about her life before Centner's Mill. "You ever see a strike, Babe?"

"Not outside a ballpark. Now, why you sittin' here jawin'

about something ain't your business when there's a sink full of dishes, and time cards to be tallied? Git, girl, and leave me to my coffee!"

That's how it was between Babe and me. She'd say something almost warm, almost inviting me into a conversation. I'd fall for it and she'd end up yelping at me to do this or do that and leave her alone.

But she never once hit me and I was determined to keep it that way. Even when she was drunk, Babe never hit me. Oh yes, Babe drank—went on a toot—exactly once a season. For no reason, every winter, spring, summer and fall, she'd go off, have a snootful, and that would be the end of it for three months. Her only explanation to me was, "I got lots to forget. Never you mind what." Who knew why, but you could have planted, harvested, tilled and replanted seed corn by her toots. I had the dates June 10 through June 25 circled on my 1918 calendar. I knew I'd be cooking for at least three out of those ten days, for it was my job to wrangle Babe out of some saloon, sober her up and keep the house until the Big Hangover wore off.

You might have noticed something else a little peculiar about the calendar I kept in my room. Father always let me have one of the Christmas calendars sent out by the head office in San Francisco. Father would get a shipment and he'd give them out with Christmas bonus checks to some of the men and the merchants in Centner's Mill. They were the kind where you could see only a day at a time. Life in a lumber camp or in the mill itself was probably viewed better that way—one day at a time.

But one day at a time wasn't enough for me. I had to look forward to another day to sometimes get through this one. So, in the lower right-hand corner of each page I would write a number. And viewed one day at a time, no one would think anything about this number. But I knew, and perhaps Babe suspected, each number had a meaning. You see, I started with the day I would turn eighteen—December 28, 1921. Then I counted the days and wrote down the number of days until my eighteenth birthday. Eighteen was the age of consent, meaning I didn't need my father's to walk out the door, travel down that rickety railroad out of Centner's Mill and never come back.

That morning, after Babe "excused" me from the table, I loaded my arms with the breakfast dishes, backed through the swinging doors and began to clean up the kitchen.

I never minded doing the dishes. I loved sinking my hands into the warm, soapy water, especially on cold mornings. The steam would rise up and cover the window over the sink and I could almost pretend I was peeking through the foggy fantasy of other worlds . . . maybe San Francisco or London. Or perhaps the light blinking at me from across the clearing was the lantern of a faraway ship—someone's ship come to rescue me. Someone—maybe Squirl—was swinging across the ship's spars, now standing at the helm, searching in the fog for me, his Cordelia.

The good thing about daydreaming is it makes the dull go faster. The dishes were done and I was now free to head to the office and collect the time cards. Maybe I'd see Squirl. Maybe I could make a slight error in calculating his hours and give him a few extra dollars to make up for what he wasn't earning out on the log booms. He'd be laid up for ten days, until the stitches came out, ten days when he'd have to take lesser wages. Maybe I could make up for the fact that he now had to run errands between the mill, the office and the town. Maybe I could help.

My father caught my error. He called me into his office. As he'd grown older, his eyesight had gotten worse, and I always hated going into his office because the brightness of his lamps made me squint. I hated reminding my father of my frailties. He hated turning down his lamps just to show me something. So I got in the habit of putting on my glasses whenever he buzzed me in.

"These don't balance," he said, tossing the bundle of time cards down on his desk.

"They don't?" I asked.

"No, they don't. I told you, you have to check your figures, Cordelia. You're off by two hours."

Actually, I was off by two and a quarter hours. I just prayed he hadn't traced it to Squirl's time card. I took the bundle and said I'd do them again.

I was nearly out of his office when he stopped me. "I don't care how good a worker that Squirl is, I tell you I'll run him out of this camp if you ever so much as glance his way!" I looked down at the time cards. On the top was Squirl's— his total hours circled in red. I should have known better than to try to fool Red Hankins with numbers.

I could have counted with the fingers of one hand the times I'd stood up to my father and still have had enough fingers left over to snap. But I was changing. I could feel it in my body. I turned and looked at him and believe me, no one does a cold stare like someone with albinism. I took my glasses off. He hated it when I did that. I simply asked why. I knew why, of course, but I wanted to hear him say it—to tell me face-to-face that I could not associate with a person of another race. I wanted him to tell it to my half-Chinese, albino face.

He pointed his finger at me and shouted, "You know why!"

I walked closer to him and said, "Yes, but I want to hear you say it!"

I was given three days' solitary in my room for that remark. Fine. Nothing made me happier. Three days of no Babe and no Father. Three days to read, dream and plan my escape, and three days of imagining Squirl and me and all the places in the world we'd go together.

5

Summer was the worst time for me. Even though Centner's Mill was nothing but shade, the sun still found me and it was sometimes a challenge to stick to the shady side of the road. More than anything I wanted to run in the sun, go to a Sunday church social, swim in the pond, let my hair hang loose. But what I wanted most was to just shed my skin like snakes do. How wonderful to wake up some morning and slither out of all this white and become someone new. Even snakes were luckier than me.

Anyway, this summer seemed the worst yet—beautiful and sunny and a daily reminder of who and what I was. Like magnets, other kids attracted their own company. I seemed to repel them. Their poles were positive. Mine were negative. Although I was a fast runner, I was now fourteen and re- quired to wear longer skirts. Although I was free on Sundays, I didn't go to church, therefore no church socials. And even though I could swim, I only did it alone and at dawn. Just the frogs, the water birds, the fish and me.

Funny how you can love doing something with someone else and just hate doing that same thing alone. So I told myself I didn't care much for swimming anyway. Maybe it was the way I'd learned.

It wasn't long after my mother had died—maybe half a year or so—that I learned how to swim. Babe had just been hired and I still slunk down low in her presence. I remember I was telling my dolls a fairy tale in my room. The door opened and Babe appeared. She had a towel over her arm and her sleeves were rolled up, as though to show off her beefy forearms.

"Yer pa says teach you to swim," she announced.

I looked up at her. "Right now? Today?" I think my eyes must have automatically filled up with tears, which meant nothing to Babe. She just went to my dresser and pulled out a pair of long johns. "Here, put these on and hope to hell they won't weigh a skinny thing like you down."

I could hear the drops of rain pinging against my window. It was late October.

"But I don't want to learn how to swim!" I cried.

"No use wailin'. What yer pa says goes. He don't want you drownin' like yer ma." She picked up the long johns, still on my bed. "You gonna put these on or am I gonna help you?"

The last thing I wanted was this beast to see my body. To hear her giant laughter shake down the rafters and echo through all of Centner's Mill. I clutched the long johns to my chest and asked her to leave while I changed.

"Thought we'd take us down to the cove. Water might be warmer there. Now, just remember, do like I tell you and we'll be done with it. No use wastin' half the day on it."

"But it's freezing out!" I cried.

"Colder the water, faster you learn."

I put the wool underwear on, wrapped my quilt about me like an Indian and appeared, mortified, downstairs.

Babe led the way. The rain was starting to come down even harder. Although it hadn't been a cold fall, I just knew how these things worked: If I survived the swim, I would first catch cold, which would turn into pneumonia, and then I would be dead by Halloween.

We must have looked comical, the Gargantua-like Babe leading the way, a towel over her arm, and a tiny me, wrapped up like a mummy, crying at my fate, following at a near run to keep up with Babe's long strides.

There was a long, narrow floating dock out over the portion of the log pond that we all referred to as the cove. Babe walked out on the dock, her weight rocking it as she went. I remember trying to keep my balance as I followed her out. The pond was calm, except for the small tidal waves the floating dock was now creating. There was a thick fog lifting off the water. Babe said that was a good sign—the water was warmer than the air. I was thinking a thick fog also meant no witnesses.

I kneeled down, put my hand in the icy water and then shot up screaming that I wasn't going in that water, I didn't care, I would take my chances about drowning, and Babe could tell my father don't worry, I'll never go anywhere near the water ever in my whole entire life.

Babe's response to that was to throw me in. She simply ripped the blanket off, spinning me around like a top, then picked me up and tossed me into the water. I was sure I was soon to meet my mother.

Babe was right about one thing: the colder the water, the faster you learn. I was frantic and dog-paddling within seconds. Screaming at Babe, choking, sputtering, crying—but swimming nonetheless.

My white skin must have been turning blue in a hurry and the last thing Babe needed on her list of accomplishments in her new job was the murdering of the boss's daughter. She kneeled on the wobbly dock, reached over and plucked me out of the water by the scruff of my long johns like a bear plucks a passing salmon out of a stream.

She landed me on the dock. I was still so mad I couldn't see. I tried to think of a name bad enough to call her, but my teeth were chattering so hard I probably would have bitten off my tongue. So I wrapped my blanket around me and started to walk back down the dock, and for the first time I saw where my small size was an advantage over her large size. The rickety dock was swaying back and forth under me. I turned and looked back at Babe. I must have looked like David sizing up Goliath. I put my feet on the edges of the dock and started to shift my weight back and forth until the dock was waving like a footbridge in a hurricane.

She looked at me, not with terror, not with anger, but with "I dare you" in her eyes.

I think all of Centner's Mill must have heard the splash when she hit the water.

I was back home, in my room, shaking from fear and cold, as I watched Babe trudge back up the path, past our house and into the cookhouse. I could hear the laughter of the men at breakfast when she appeared.

I knew I was done for.

But she never ever referred to the swimming lesson she gave me or the physics lesson I gave her. Nor did my father.

Anyway, that's how I learned to swim. And that's also probably why I never found it particularly enjoyable, especially alone, which is also why I preferred the woods. Besides, in the woods, I was never really alone.

It was only natural that on Sundays—when the loggers were either sleeping it off or down in Aberdeen or in church with their families, when the mill was closed down and the town was quiet—I would take to the woods. In summer, I had the excuse of going berry picking—although it seemed, as often as not, I'd come back with my bucket empty and my gloves unstained.

Luckily for me, on my eleventh birthday I'd gotten another excuse to escape on Sundays . . . a sketch pad. I would go up into the hills above Centner's Mill and sketch. No one asked to see my sketches when I returned, even though I usually made several. The problem with my eyesight meant that I couldn't copy detailed landscapes, so I'd just make someplace up. I liked my way better.

On this particular Sunday, when my three days of solitary were over, I needed to escape more than ever. Especially since I had seen Squirl take the Flume Trail up the hillside the last three Sundays. I packed a lunch and a few art supplies and headed out.

6

There is something about the smell of the woods on a hot day. It's almost as though you can smell, maybe even taste, the coolness found in the shade. The sun comes through the treetops like piercing swords of light, stabbing the piney floor and ever so briefly illuminating it. The sweet smell of the undergrowth—new fronds springing from dead logs, salal and Oregon grape—mixes with the smells of pine and cedar and hemlock. When I was young, I used to wonder if trees had thoughts and if they did, what were they? When I was very young and my father and mother worked in a logging camp, not a mill, I really, truly used to think it was the tree that cried, *"Timber!"* when it was cut and falling down. But it wasn't screeched as a warning. It was a death cry.

The woods frightened me then. But it wasn't just the stories of the mythical monsters—like the Hodog and the Sasquatch. I was as puny a coward as there ever was. I was even scared of the knotty pine on the floor of our logging camp tent. I thought the knots were the eyes of the trees, staring coldly up at me. I could never step on one of the knots. I know it was stupid of me, but I think I was probably nine or so before I ever totally turned my back on a tree.

But now I loved the forest and I knew every square inch of the hills that embraced Centner's Mill. Half of the trails I had blazed myself and had secretly named, although I didn't want to get too chummy with the trees around them. We all knew their time was coming. But as long as the logging camps higher up in the hills kept the pond full and the mill running, as long as the train tracks could be laid and the trestles built, my little forest was safe.

I took the Flume Trail, so named because it paralleled the log flume that cut a winding path down Logue's Mountain. This flume ran five miles—one of the longest on the West Coast, so I'd heard the men brag. I thought it must have circled the mountain five or six times, from what the loggers said.

The progression of a fallen tree was this: One minute you're standing, maybe a couple of hundred years old, the next you're on the ground, dead. Then men are on you, walking and measuring your length, lopping off your branches and sawing you in sections. No respect, just income. Then someone hooks huge clamps around you and drags your sections high into the air, as though you are dancing along a high wire, which in a way, you are. The wire connects with the high pole—one of your cousins picked for its strength and height. Then you travel down this wire and are plopped onto the bed of a train. If you've come from higher up, oxen pull you along a skid track. If you've grown close to the track, you ride the train. Once all of you is loaded on the bed of the cars, you travel down this rickety track, pulled along with a steam donkey, sort of like a train engine.

A few miles down the mountain, the tram comes to a stop and you are tipped off the bed of the car, and then you roll down a smooth hill, where you come to a stop. It's here you are measured and graded for value. This decided, you are given another push by a loader, again down a grade, and then you finally feel water. This is a small holding pond created by damming one of the mountain streams. You are quickly corralled into a chute, which becomes the flume. Then, one section at a time, you are floated down this flume. If one of your branches hasn't been trimmed flush, you might catch on something and cause a jam or worse yet, damage the flume. If you cause too much trouble and fall off the flume, good riddance—for that is where you'll rot. You won't cascade into the log pond down in Centner's Mill, nor will you be sorted and graded again, nor will you be chosen to ride the conveyor belt up and into the mill, nor will you have any value or worth. It's over—back to the forest floor. If you're lucky, a bird will drop a seed in your bark and you'll spawn another tree someday. But that's the best you can hope for if you've been a troublemaker tree. Better do what you're told—stay on the mark, toe the line, and at least that way you can be milled into something someone will cherish someday—a thing of beauty like a rocking chair or carved wainscotting or a baby's cradle. Or maybe you'll end up being something important, like a ship's mast or an aeroplane's wing or plank track for racing automobiles. The possibilities are endless.

But today was Sunday and everyone, trees included, had the day off. All that ran through the flume was a lazy stream of water and an occasional fingerling salmon or trout, cheating its way downstream. Water gushed like a river through the flume only when they opened the sluice gates in the holding pond to carry the logs downhill.

I chose the highest point, the point where I could see the town below, the log pond, and the winding flume, to set up my sketching supplies. My plan was to sit in the shade and start to sketch. That way, if and when Squirl came along the Flume Trail, he and I would meet.

I read, I ate, I drank lemonade, I sketched, I daydreamed and I fell asleep.

The sound of footsteps on the trail from below snapped me awake. I quickly sat up, pulled my glasses up by the string around my neck and put them on. I straightened my hat and pretended to be as startled to see him as he was to see me.

"Oh. Hello," I said, demurely looking at him over my sketch pad. I knew my knitted glove must have been imprinted on my cheek from my nap.

"Nice day, today, eh?" he asked.

I said yes and smiled with my lips closed.

Squirl came up and stood behind me. He asked if he could take a closer look at my sketch. Embarrassed, I hesitated a little, but he reached down and took the pad off my knee-easel. He looked at my sketch, then back down at the log pond, as if to compare the likeness. There wasn't any. I had drawn a picture of a large city—who knows which one—maybe Chicago, maybe New York, maybe San Francisco. There was a skyline of tall buildings—some probably far taller than they actually were. I'd drawn in two aeroplanes flying by. And there was a large body of water lapping the shore. All great cities were on the water, I knew that.

Squirl handed me back the sketch. "Seattle," he announced.

I looked at the sketch, lifted my glasses to get a clearer look, then half-asked, half-agreed, "Seattle."

"Sure," Squirl said, now kneeling down next to me and pointing to my sketch. I wanted to lean away so his face wasn't so close to mine. I pushed my glasses against my nose. He pointed to the sketch and continued, "Been there a hundred times. There's the Smith Tower there, there's Fisherman's Terminal, and that's where they bring in the Mosquito Fleet, right there."

No one was more surprised than me to see I'd correctly drawn Seattle.

Then he pointed to a row of trees along the waterfront and added, "But I guess it's been a while since you was there. Not a tree left standin' on the Seattle waterfront."

I took the sketch and closed the book on it and the well-treed Seattle waterfront.

Squirl sat down and said, "You never been there, have you?"

I looked out over the pond—I'd seen a billion logs, but had never seen what became of them. I'd only dreamed, imagined, sketched.

"No," I said. "Got the rest of my life to see Seattle. Other towns. The world."

"Just how long you plannin' on livin'?" he asked back, peeling bark off a twig and tossing the pieces downhill.

"Long enough to see what I want to see," I replied.

Then he gave me his odd, mocking smile and said, "Hope you're planning on makin' your way in the world with something other'n drawin'."

I couldn't hold back my smile. Making my way? As though I'd ever be let loose to make my way to the outskirts of town, let alone the world.

"Tell me about it. Seattle," I said.

Squirl looked out over the pond and I watched his face as he spoke. His dark eyes came alive as he told me about the wharf's line of masted ships, going to and coming from all over the world, the avenues of automobiles and streetcars, the buildings with elevators and the Bill Boeing aeroplanes flying overhead. I sat mesmerized as he told me about the streets, the people, the crime, the excitement, and how, every so often when he'd had enough of working, he'd cut his tail-holt and take his fortune to Seattle and squander it all on cheap bootleg booze, expensive women and gambling. And how, someday, he'd sail off to the South Seas, make another fortune on copra and black pearls and then come back and do it all over again.

But I hadn't joined him for the South Seas. I was still back in Seattle. "How can a woman be expensive?" I asked. "You mean she's got rich tastes?"

Squirl must have heard something in my voice—a longing, an evil curiosity. He lowered his voice and spoke in a velvety tone, as though to tempt me or to test my courage. "Yeah. They got rich tastes. You know, they got *places* in Seattle. Places where *everything's* expensive. If you know what I mean. There's this place outside Seattle. To the west. Luna Park," Squirl continued, all grins and teasing. "Ever hear of Luna Park?"

I shook my head. By the look on his face, I wanted to know more.

"They got everything there. *Everything.* Most especially they got Cousin Sally's."

"You got kin there?"

"*Everyone's* kin at Cousin Sally's," he replied. He watched my reaction, then went on. "Luna Park is this sort of . . .

well, an amusement park. Only, if you know where to look and if you got connections—I got connections—you can find more amusement than just roller coasters and sideshows and all."

I had no idea what he was talking about. "Like what?" I asked, knowing I sounded skeptical.

"I'd tell you, but you'd just faint dead away and then I'd have to haul you down off the hill."

It was then I knew he was teasing me. "You're plain lyin'," I said, gathering my skirts around me and putting away my sketch pad.

Squirl rolled back and looked at the sky and seemed to be talking to the clouds overhead. "Maybe I am. Maybe I ain't. You'll just have to see for yourself one day."

All I could answer was, "If you're born a liar, you'll die a liar."

"That's all the world needs—another high thinker," Squirl said, my insult running off his forehead, down his wonderful dark cheeks and into the grass under his head. "You ever get to Seattle, you just go find Cousin Sally's at Luna Park. Tell 'em Squirl sent you and they'll fix you right up."

But that prospect, the vision of me in that place, made him laugh. "On second thought, maybe a girl like you'd be better off staying right here in Centner's Mill."

"Only for . . . ," I started, closing my eyes to visualize the number on my calendar. "Only for exactly one thousand two hundred and seventy-six days. In exactly one thousand two hundred and seventy-six days I'm eighteen and off this mountain."

He started to calculate, keeping his eyes on mine. "You're eighteen on December twenty-seventh, 1921?"

"No. The twenty-eighth."

"Then you forgot 1920 is a leap year. Add a day."

"Oh. One more day. Okay, so in one thousand two hundred and seventy-*seven* days I'm off this mountain. How'd you calculate that in your head, anyway?"

He shrugged and said, "Just one of my God-given talents. Not much good for anything but gamblin'. Anyway, that's too long a time for anyone to wait for anything or anybody." He looked at me, grinned and added, "And countin' days ain't my style. I live for today. And when you live like I do, today's all you need."

Why hadn't I ever thought of that?

"Hey, enough of this high thinkin'," he said, jumping to his feet.

"Got to go. Got me a bet goin'," he said, indicating the town downhill.

"A bet? On Sunday? You know what God would say about that."

"I sure do. He'd say I was plumb crazy and dumb to boot for bettin' on a Sunday when everyone knows there ain't no serious cash in a mill town on a Sunday, unless you're bettin' with the barkeep."

"So what's this bet?" I asked cautiously, wondering if it had anything to do with me.

"I bet Arty—you know ol' Arty, the mule skinner—that I could make it from the cookhouse, get up to the log dump, pick up a grading ticket from the scaling shed and make it back by Sunday dinner at three. He's timing me now."

I thought *he was* plumb crazy for such a bet. It was nearly noon and he had a four-mile hike uphill ahead of him. Then he had to get into the scaling shed, grab a ticket and trek back down, which sometimes was harder going than the uphill part.

"You better get going," I warned.

"Yeah, suppose so."

"How much you bet?" I asked, in agony that he was going to have to leave soon.

"Ten bucks."

"Then you *really* better get going."

"I ain't worried," he said with a grin of confidence that I'd already come to adore. "Got the whole thing all planned out. I can make it by two-thirty, latest."

"That I'd like to see," I said.

"Then come with me," he said. "Keep me honest."

Although I looked like a runt, I was part mountain goat, my legs being small but strong. Gravity was my friend while hiking uphill. So I stood up, dusted off my skirts and said, "Maybe I just will."

"No whinin', though. You get tired, you just head back down," he warned.

I tossed the remnants of my picnic into my rucksack, slung it on my back and said, "I don't get tired and I don't whine."

He led the way up the path and I was thrilled to follow. The last thing I was thinking about was what anyone, my father especially, would say.

7

Squirl *had* planned it all out. I thought I knew the high trail better than just about anyone, but he showed me some short-cuts that he himself must have blazed. By switching back and then taking a steeper route, we shaved maybe a half mile off our journey. I didn't whine once.

But along our way, I asked Squirl why he didn't just get a grading ticket from one of the loggers or from me—spare himself all this work. I could get him a ticket in one minute flat down at the mill. He stopped and looked back down at me on the trail below him as though that was the most stupid thing he'd ever heard of, and maybe wasn't I a little evil-minded to even suggest that he cheat? Naturally, I wouldn't have cheated, but I assumed Squirl would. In a heartbeat. He explained to me that the bet had been planned for two weeks now. The ticket he was to pick up was a special ticket—one that the man he'd betted with had tacked in the scaling shed. It was no good bringing back just any grading ticket. So it turned out that I wasn't stupid for suggesting he might cheat, I was stupid for thinking it was that easy.

When we arrived up at the scaling shed, Squirl pulled out the key to the door, opened it, disappeared and then came back out with the ticket.

"See there?" he said, showing it to me. It was a typical grading ticket—just boxes where the lengths and widths of logs could be tallied along with their grades. I'd probably calculated a million of them.

I turned it over and there was the signature of the man, Arty Hostetter, along with the words "Ten Bucks." I looked at the shadows we were casting and suggested maybe we should start back downhill.

Squirl looked at me and said, "What's your hurry? We have plenty of time."

I was so stupid. I had no instincts. I didn't know that edginess I was feeling was because I was standing in a camp that I had only seen bustling with men and logs and activity and noise, which was now as silent as the gliding hawk overhead. The empty log pond lapped gently against the graveled shore. I was now able to hear the rustle of the treetops in the easy breeze instead of the deafening squeal of the tram brakes, the moan of the skidders, the crash of the logs. I was alone with Squirl, the boy I'd been forbidden to even gaze at or talk to—let alone share this silence with.

I looked at him and again suggested we get back. I said ten bucks was a lot of money and we'd come so far, so fast, and I had to be home by three o'clock, so maybe we'd better start.

Then it happened. He said I was a curious little thing. Sooner or later, I knew he was going to want to know how I came to be this odd. It was the story of my life. I told him my heritage. I did not mention I was the boss's daughter. If he didn't already know, no use spooking him off.

"Never met me an albino. Well, that ain't exactly true. I did see a white deer once. She was so dang pretty, I just set my rifle down and let her pass." We were now sitting on a log next to the holding pond. He touched a wisp of my hair from under my cap. "Saw me one, but never met me one."

Oh Lord, he was going to kiss me! And I had no idea how I knew. It wasn't as though I'd *ever* seen my father kiss Babe. All the knowledge I had about things of this sort came from Brontë, Byron and other old writers whose books I was allowed to read.

I watched his lips come closer until they lightly touched mine. I didn't move but knew I should. I might have put my head back a little at the touch of his lips, but I didn't protest. I knew I was going to hell anyway. Babe had warned me of the rewards of evil thinking. Might as well go for a kiss as a thought.

Squirl smiled at me and said that was nice. I was breathless, so I couldn't reply. He kissed me again, this time leaning into me more. I almost lost my balance as I leaned back. He kept pressing forward until my back was arching to keep my balance. He leaned into me even more until I finally fell backward on the log. He fell on top of me. We rolled off and onto the soft dirt. My glasses came half off, my cap slipped back, and he saw me as face-to-face as it gets. His full weight was upon me and I didn't know to object. I didn't want to object. This was Squirl.

He smiled at me and I found my heart beating against his, curious how our two bodies seemed to fit together like pieces of a puzzle . . . almost seamless and in unison. Another kiss, harder and warm and pushing down. Then he just looked at me—took my glasses, studied me, ran his hand down my odd little face. "You're so . . ."

Here it comes, I thought.

"You're so . . . strange, you're beautiful. Your eyes . . . they're dancing a jig. You're really amazing. You're almost ugly. But you're so beautiful. There's just one thing I need to know."

Oh, so *now* it comes, I thought. But I asked, "What?"

"Your name."

"Cordy," I replied, trying not to smile in my relief.

"Cordy?" he asked, his eyebrows arching as he spoke. "Now, would that be as in a cordy of wood, or a cordy on the piano, or as in 'Give a man enough cordy and he'll hang himself'?"

I covered my mouth as I laughed. "None," I said. "It's Cordelia."

"Cordelia," he repeated, as though he'd never ever heard that name before. "Cor-deal-ee-ah."

It had never sounded so beautiful as when Squirl said it.

He kissed me again and got up, pulling me up with him. I think I was dizzy. Maybe it was the brightness on my eyes.

He ran his fingers through his hair to get it out of his face. He seemed a little out of breath, and all the while he was studying me.

"What are you looking at?" I asked.

"I'm thinkin'," he said. "You never been kissed like that, have you?"

"Never been *kissed*," I confessed; much too honest, much too fast.

"You scared bein' alone with me up here? Gettin' kissed

for the first time? Cordy?" he asked, coming closer and watching my mouth as I replied, "No."

"Maybe you should be. Ain't your folks taught you better?" He put his arm around my waist, pulled me to him, caught me off guard, nearly crushed my glasses.

His embrace was now forceful, his kiss open-lipped. His hands stroked my back. I looked at him and our eyes met; then he closed his and so I closed mine. Then he let me go, as though it was me holding him. He was shaking.

He reached to touch a section of my undone white hair, and said, "Maybe we better start down."

I nodded, not at all sure what was happening between us. I put my glasses back on and started to walk down the trail, tucking my hair under my cap. I didn't know exactly what else to do. But he didn't follow.

I was just below the flume when I heard a sudden gush of water. I looked up and the sluice gate was open and now running full force. Water splashed down on me and I went back up the hill.

"Hey!" Squirl called out as I came back into the clearing. "Where you goin'?"

I came closer and for a moment I thought he was standing on the water. But he was on a raft made up of three logs— two larger ones with a smaller one on top—floating along the shore, perfectly balanced.

"I'm going back down," I called to him. "Remember? The bet? Ten bucks?"

"Then get back up here!" he called, his smile flashing.

I hiked my skirt up and ran back.

"I came up here last Sunday and made me this raft. Kept it hid over there," he called out.

It didn't take a genius to figure out what he was planning. Again, I was speechless. I guess that comes from being raised the way I was. Speechless seemed to be my natural state for all new experiences.

"Go get me a peavey," he ordered, pointing to the scaling shed where they were kept. Peaveys are pike poles—you know, those long spikes the boom men use to poke the logs along. I grabbed one and held it out to him.

"You can't do that," I warned. But he tugged on the pole as though to urge me into the water. I let go.

"Do what?" he asked, now groaning against the peavey until the raft began to move.

"Do what I think you're going to do."

"Which is what?" Another last shove and the raft was gliding slowly toward the sluice gate. With a catlike balance, Squirl stood, poking the peavey into the sand to shove the raft along.

I walked on the shore alongside him. "Squirl, it's against the law!" I shouted out to him.

He looked at me like I was crazy. "The *law*? It's against every goddamn rule in every logging camp, but it ain't against the *law*."

"They'll run you out on a rail!"

"Not if they don't find out!"

I ran ahead to the sluice gate to pull the lever that would close it and stop the log. "Leave that alone, Cordy! I'm doing this!"

It took all my body weight pulling back the lever. The water came to a crashing halt, splashing all over me. Squirl's raft also came to a sudden halt, catapulting him off the flume head. He somersaulted into the trail below. The peavey went flying through the air.

Squirl glared at me over the flume, his hair all plastered down on his face. I was drenched too, and we both broke out laughing at the sight we made. He climbed up on the flume again, his jaw clenched and his face breaking into a determined smile. He stood on the sluice gate, holding the lever in one hand. He held the other hand out to me. "Lift those glasses and look me in the eyes and tell me you ain't never wanted to ride the flume."

I lifted my glasses and looked him in the eyes. It hurt, but I knew nothing but eye-to-eye would do with Squirl. "I have never wanted to ride the flume," I said.

"Liar."

I looked at his outstretched hand and realized I would have ridden the flume through the gates of hell for him. I bent down, scooped up my long skirts, brought them through my legs and tucked them into my belt, giving me puffy pantaloons. I took his hand and sat astride the raft.

He grabbed the peavey and said, "Here, hold this and don't hit me in the head with it."

He told me to scoot back, for when he pushed the lever he was going to have to jump quickly and land perfectly in front of me or I'd be riding down solo.

"As though I need you to steer this thing," I mumbled.

"Yeah, we're pretty much going where it wants to go."

I was telling myself to get off the raft while I could, that if this Squirl daredevil wanted to kill himself that was fine, but why take me with him? Oh hell, my father was going to kill me anyway.

"So, how many times have you done this?" I asked, suddenly unable to swallow and wondering why I didn't use the outhouse at the scaling shed while I had the chance.

"Well, never," Squirl admitted, pushing the lever open.

Then, as the water started to leak through and the raft began to move, he added, "But I've watched a million logs do it. And the flume inspector rode it just last weeeeeeeeek. . . ."

It was too late to change my mind. The sluice gate was open. Squirl leaped aboard and seized the peavey. My arms were wrapped around him at least six times and we were off.

Naturally, Squirl had called it right. I was lying when I told
him I hadn't always dreamed of riding the flume. I may have
been unlike any other kid in any other way, but all kids
around a lumber camp want to ride the flume. Few try, even
fewer succeed, but all kids talk about it, plan on it, brag
about it—but it's all just "someday." This *was* someday. The
immediate here and now.

My first thought in the immediate here and now was the
logging pond. Surely Squirl wouldn't be attempting this
stunt if he knew there was a bed of logs at the end. Then
we'd go catapulting off the flume and fly out and over and
splat on a log boom. I was so busy worrying about the end
of our ride, it never occurred to me to think about the
dangers that were waiting at every turn. Until Squirl brought
them to my attention, that is.

"You afraid of heights?" he asked, just as we were approaching the trestle that connected the walls of Dead Bear

Canyon. From atop our log raft, from the narrow flume, it seemed like the canyon floor was a mile below.

"Would it make any difference?" I asked through clenched teeth. Clenched to keep them from chattering—chattering from the freezing cold of the mountain water on my legs and chattering from terror. I clutched Squirl's middle and hoped he couldn't feel my fear.

"Oh God," was his reply, which really wasn't what I wanted to hear. His back stiffened as he looked ahead and I dared to peer around him. "Who left *that* there?" he cried. I barely saw what he was talking about when he ordered, "Hang on! We're going to hit!" He took his peavey and braced it in front of our raft. "Why here, why here, why here?" he chanted nervously as we came on the jam of logging debris some lazy logger had tossed onto the flume rather than drag to the slash pile. Even I knew that was a cardinal sin against any logging operation. We slammed into the debris, and water cascaded over the side of the flume. On the good side, we knocked the jam loose and sped it down the flume ahead of us. But the force of the hit knocked us both forward. Without Squirl to steady me, I lost my balance and fell into the water. Odd at a time like that you think about your glasses. Thank God I had them connected with a string, so when they fell off they didn't go far. Squirl had other problems to think about. He'd fallen off, too, but was river rat through and through. He anchored his legs against the flume, then used his peavey to hook our raft by the chain and pushed, holding it against the gentle current.

But he was starting to lose his toe-holt. "You climb back on while I hold her," Squirl said, spitting out water. There I was, on the verge of disaster, noticing how handsome he was. "Don't look down. Just get on the raft."

"Then what?" I asked. I could see by the reddening of his face and the sudden burst of current that he wasn't about to explain anything. God, the water was cold.

"Can you put a leg out against the flume and hold her?" Squirl called up to me once I'd carefully slithered back on the raft. He was losing his grip and I felt the raft start to move forward. I did as I was told. He handed the peavey to me. I was able to hook it over the side of the flume and hold us in place long enough for Squirl to climb aboard before our raft gushed forward and crushed him. He took the peavey but the sharp end had anchored in the flume.

"Oh, great!" he shouted.

He yanked up with such a force that I thought he'd surely go catapulting over the other side when it came loose, which it did, but he kept his balance. An old, rotted section of the flume broke loose and fell into the canyon. The silence until it hit on the rocks below was a reminder of how high up we were. The water, now deeper, angrier behind us, flowed over the top and splattered on the trees and rocks below.

Squirl gave another shove against the flume and we were back on our way. I dared a glance behind us at the rotten, broken section of the flume, but I didn't dare to imagine my father's wrath.

"Too bad we won't be able to tell anyone about this," Squirl said back to me. After a few seconds, he pointed and I looked behind us. "That damn flume inspector should have found that rotted section!"

I started to shake out of fear, out of cold, out of the terror of knowing what our prank was going to cost my father.

On the good side, Squirl reckoned we were halfway down the mountain.

I asked him if he expected any other surprises.

"Never expect a surprise. Takes the whole purpose outa life," he answered. I couldn't see his face, of course, but I know he was grinning, mentally spending his ten-dollar winnings.

Of course, the worst was still ahead.

The final chute into the log pond was about four stories high. I used to love to sit and watch the logs as they came speeding down the flume and then leaped, fearless, into the air for a silent moment until they crashed into the water below. Usually the logs would hit the water with their blunt, newly cut ends and that would cause a giant spray of water. Some logs would just gracefully fly for a distance, maybe even spiral a few revolutions midair, then land, *slap!* flat on the water. The equivalent of a human belly flop. Occasionally logs landed with giant groans on the backs of other logs, and large chunks of wood came flying off from the force. Oh. *I* could be one of those clumsy, unlucky logs. Once again, all I could think about was our final destination . . . the log pond.

"You *can* swim, can't you?" Squirl asked, as though he could read my mind.

Nervously, I replied, "Why do you ask?"

"You *can* swim, *can't you?*" he asked again, only louder and very urgent.

I thought of my mother drowning in that pond. I thought of Babe trying to drown *me* in that pond. "Do you think I'd be stupid enough to do this if I couldn't?" I asked back.

"I don't know," Squirl said, "even getting on this thing with me was pretty stupid."

Gee, I wished he hadn't said that. I wished his voice was low, in control and commanding—the way it had been when he challenged me to this idiocy. Instead, his voice was now higher and maybe even as shaky as mine.

We came around the last bend and we could see the log pond and Centner's Mill below. The last leg—almost straight down. We gathered speed as though the water that carried us along was eager to join the pond. I held on to Squirl tight and locked my wrists.

"So what's the plan?" I asked, probably shattering his eardrum.

"What plan? There's no *plan*. We're going into the pond!" he yelped back. He held his peavey in front of him.

I must have tightened my grip. He must have finally felt my fear. He put his hand back on my leg, rubbed it and said, "As soon as we're airborne, try to push off the raft. The only thing you have to worry about is hitting your head on something."

That and my father, I thought. Well, if this was to be my last day on earth, then I had no complaints. Squirl had kissed me again and again. And he had saved my life on the trestle—without his strength, his balance, his calm, I'd be frozen there still, looking down over the side, unable to move until a giant log came and put me out of my misery.

We were going faster, faster. It was now somehow thrilling, not frightening. Just as we approached the end, Squirl tossed his peavey high into the air. I never would have thought of that. I would have clutched the thing like a drowning person clutches a straw and then it could have come out of my hands, turned around in midair, come back down and pierced me through my heart.

As we hit the air, Squirl issued a full-of-life *"Yaaaaaahoooooo."* I think I screamed. The raft continued on its way and it might have been an hour, maybe two, before I hit the water. My skirts had become all tangled and I thought how comical, how unladylike I must look—my skirts nearly above my head, Sunday pink bloomers flapping, my white hair undone and flying as I splashed into the water.

As I went under the surface, the sounds immediately changed from air noises to water noises—those muted, blunt sounds as your ears fill. I must have sunk two or three fathoms. I was sure I was going to touch bottom, maybe even stick in it.

Finally, I started to swim up—grasping armfuls of water, heading toward the light above. Then my head started to hurt. No, nothing had hit me—Squirl had found a handful of my hair and was pulling me up.

I surfaced, gasping for air and facing Squirl in the water.

"Good thing for your white hair," he shouted at me. "Don't ever cut it."

I rubbed my scalp. He was wild with exuberance. Couldn't stop talking all the way to shore. My skirts were hopelessly tangled by then and I tired very quickly. It was his suggestion for me to undo the waistband and swim out of my skirt. I hadn't survived the ride just to drown because of proprieties. Besides, any reputation I might have had was spoiled anyway. I kicked out of my skirts and let them sink.

We climbed out of the water behind the mill and sat, exhausted, freezing, laughing, on the shore. Squirl's face, in his victory, was worth it all. He looked at me—the half-drowned white rat—and I looked at him—the glistening hero. He kissed me hard, laughing. The laughing stopped and the kiss was now filled with purpose. I put my arms around him and we must have looked like two otters, entwined and rolling in the mud. We nearly slid back down the bank and into the water. The smells and sounds of water, mud, sweat, close death and life meshed gloriously.

He finally stopped kissing me and looked down at me. "God, you're a mess." I could tell he was trying to hold back his laughter.

I hated being forced to smile, to show my yellow teeth, but I couldn't help it. He joined me and I thought the sound of our combined laughter was the most wonderful, consonant sound in the world.

We made quite a sight. Wet, muddy, flushed, victorious. I hadn't put one ounce of thought into how I was going to explain myself, should either Babe or my father catch me sneaking back into the house. My skirts were probably resting peacefully on the bottom of the pond. My rucksack was nothing more than a heavy canvas bag full of drenched sketches. My glasses were, thank God, still safe around my neck. My hat was who knows where. My face, under the mud, was blushing from our—what was it called?—our encounter.

Squirl had offered me his hand as we stood up and we kept holding hands, walking along the shore of the pond toward the mill. It's so hard to describe my heart—it's like I had cheated death and in my bravery, had found new life. Then finally, I remembered who I was, where I was. I looked around and up. I stopped cold.

Squirl turned. "What?"

"My father," I barely uttered.

Squirl followed my glance to the breakwater by the mill, then said, "Uh-uh, worse, Cordy. That's Red Hankins. The boss man."

"Who is . . . my father," I said.

Squirl let go of my hand.

9

Done for.

This is how deep my love was for Squirl: All I could think about was him. About the pay he would probably be docked as punishment, about the stitches in his cut hand having been ripped off somewhere between the logjam on the trestle and the plunge, about his escaping the wrath of my father before three o'clock, when the time limit on the bet wore off and he'd be out ten bucks.

I had only to glance up into my father's raging eyes to know I was to go home, change clothes and await my fate in my room. My father made no effort to help cloak me. My wet bloomers clung to my skin and I felt naked and exposed. It was Squirl who took off his soaking hickory shirt and handed it to me to wrap around my waist. I could tell by my father's face that he objected, but I grabbed the shirt, quickly put it around myself and ran the shady backyard trails toward home. I wondered if I'd ever see Squirl alive again.

It wasn't until I crept up onto our back porch and sat

down, exhausted and freezing, to unbutton my shoes, that I began to think of myself. Tears appeared from nowhere. I was trembling so hard, I could barely get my fingers to work. I thought of the wonderful afternoon, of Squirl's inquisitive kisses, his warm body on mine, his laugh as we conquered the flume. The adventure. The terror. How can life be so wonderful one minute and so horrible the next? I was thinking. Why couldn't that flume run all the way to Seattle, where we could fly off into some other world where no one knew us, where fathers didn't look down from on high, and where giant stepmothers didn't appear out of nowhere to yank you up by your collar and whirl you around?

"You tell me what you been up to, girl!" Babe demanded, her huge, ugly face close to mine, her deep voice almost growling at me.

I had no composure to gather, I had no dignity left to cloak me. I was a muddy, soaking, trembling nothing, cowering, unable to utter a defense or explanation or excuse or even a lie. I turned to run and she grabbed a sleeve of Squirl's shirt and snapped me back. I pulled against the shirt, heard a rip, and it was Babe's now to inspect, wad up and throw with such force into the floorboards of the porch that tiny droplets of dirty water flew back up and spotted us both, increasing Babe's wrath.

Of course, she could snap me in half like kindling. I ran into the kitchen, up the service stairs, down the hall, and slammed my bedroom door. Why bother locking it, knowing Babe could and probably would tear the house apart beam by panel by joist to get to me?

But she didn't come up looking for me. Nor did my father. I didn't dare risk being caught off guard by taking a bath, although I wanted more than anything to sink into a tub of hot water and self-pity. Instead, I steamed some towels and quickly sponged off, with my disgraced back to the mirror.

That's when I first noticed the blood. It was on the towel. I didn't think anything of it except how odd I hadn't felt the cut when it happened. Oh well, in the glory of the day . . . I inspected my body for the wound. Found nothing. I had gotten through the adventure without so much as a sliver. And yet, when I ran the towel between my legs—blood.

The terror I felt ran through my whole body—more than just my heart leaping. It was as though some chemical was surging through my veins, touching every nerve, every cell. This is how people must feel when the doctor tells them they have exactly one week left to live, when the logging foreman comes knocking at your door with the camp chaplain to tell you your son is dead, when you look up from the foxhole in France and hear the bullet coming at your face. I was bleeding internally. I was going to bleed to death that night, in my bed, scorned by my father, never to see my love again, and with no one to blame but myself.

Could a doctor even help? In the logging business, men died all the time of what they called "their insides injuries." All the time you heard about men bleeding to death internally and now I was doing it. What a delicate body I must have. This somehow calmed me—as though something like this was bound to happen sooner or later. It probably had something to do with my mixed race heritage. Maybe Chinese insides break apart easier than Caucasian insides. And now this was my fate. No wonder my father had worked so hard to protect me.

I dressed in flannels, put a clean towel between my legs, and weakly climbed into bed. I vaguely recalled finding blood a few months ago, but it was such a trivial amount I'd easily convinced myself it was nothing. I cursed myself for ignoring such a warning sign. Now this. Sooner or later, someone—my father, Babe, the doctor, the undertaker—surely someone would come to help me die. Maybe Squirl would find me and hold my hand until the end. Then throw himself off the trestle in the agony and guilt of my untimely death.

I heard the telephone ring downstairs and I knew it was my father calling Babe from the mill office. Had to be. It was Sunday and our telephone almost never rang on a Sunday.

I was right, for the next sound I heard was Babe's tread on the stairs. You always got fair warning with Babe.

She opened my door, saw me in bed, glared furiously at me and then went into my bathroom with her load of clean towels.

It would soon be over, I thought. I'd made no effort to hide the bloody towel and now she, my father, all who had ever done me any wrong, would soon be sorry as I lay dying.

She came out of the bathroom holding one of the bloody towels out in front of her. "What is this?" she demanded, showing me the towel.

"Blood," I answered weakly.

"I can see it's blood! Where'd it come from?"

"Me," I replied.

She tossed the towel on my bed so hard I felt a small gust of wind. "Don't you dare sass me, missy! Now, you tell me what happened today and you tell me right now!"

I managed to sit myself up a little. If I was frightened to lie in my room alone, feeling the life ooze out of my body, then seeing Babe's outraged face towering above me nearly gave me a heart attack.

It was more than I could take. I buried my head in my

pillow and cried and cried. If I dared to dream she would scoop me into her giant arms and rock me, soothe me, mother me, it was all just that—a dream. Instead, she shook me by the shoulder and again demanded I tell her what had happened on the mountain that day with Squirl.

Squirl? How did he get into this? I turned and looked at Babe at the mention of his name. "Why?" I asked.

She again showed me the bloody towel. "Did he . . . did he make . . . *love* . . . to you?" It was as though she wasn't able to get the word "love" off her tongue and through her lips and into the air for me to hear.

Love? How could she possibly know? I was blubbering now into my pillow. Here I was dying. And even on my deathbed, I was being tormented by Babe.

I didn't know how to even begin to answer.

Babe grabbed me by an arm, pulled me up and closer to her face, and demanded to know if he had "spoilt" me.

I had no idea what my bleeding to death from my crushed, delicate internal organs could have to do with being "spoilt." I really didn't think Babe knew how seriously injured I was. I pulled the towel out from between my legs and showed her the bloodstain which, to my amazement, was now quite small. Her face seemed to explode and she asked if Squirl had done that to me and I guess, in a way, he had.

I nodded weakly, unable to lie. "Will I die?" I asked.

She didn't answer. Then I confessed, "I bled once before, but it was so small, I . . . I . . . Do you think it's maybe . . . cancer?"

Babe ran her hand over her face, thinking, as she looked down on me. "No, you ain't gonna die!" she said harshly. "Though you may wish you could!" Then she left my room, went down the hall and came back with some torn-up rags

64

and showed me what to do with them. No doctor, no priest, just rags. Well, looks like Babe was going to be Babe right up to the end, I thought.

I couldn't stop crying. Babe, in a rare moment of pity, looked down on me and said, "Stop blubberin', girl. Cryin' ain't gonna do no good. Alls this means is you're a woman now and old enough to have a baby, which you just might if what you said 'bout that Squirl is true! And you better not say nothin' to nobody 'bout this, neither!"

A baby? What did a baby have to do with this?

She reached into her pocket and handed me a shaker of pepper.

"What's this for?" I asked, taking it from her.

"You best start sneezin' and sneezin' hard," she explained.

I looked at the shaker, carefully sniffed it, but no sneeze. "Why do I have to do this?" I asked.

She looked at me like I was as dumb as a rock. "Don't you know nothin'? Sneezin's your only hope. You know what's good for you, you'll sneeze till the cows come home!"

Babe left the room, slamming the door behind her. I opened the pepper shaker and poured some into my hand. I sneezed, cried, sneezed some more, and got the hiccups. If sneezing was good, then hiccups might even help.

When I put all the pieces together, I decided I would rather die of crushed organs or even cancer. As it was, I was going to suffer a fate much worse than bleeding to death.

It was obvious. As plain as the flat nose on my face.

I was pregnant.

10

My diagnosis was confirmed when Babe came back upstairs and told me quite bluntly I had to stay in bed for a few days. Oh, I could walk about my room some, read some, do some needlework, yes, it would be a good time to catch up on the mending. I was too terrified to say anything but nodded helplessly while she loomed over me and plopped her sewing basket down at my feet.

Fate. Of all the imaginings my mind had gotten me into and out of back when I was a child, I could never have imagined this. How could this be happening to me? How indeed. I was fourteen. I had been raised in a lumber camp with all sorts of men coming and going. Men don't tell girls these things. Women do. So why hadn't someone—my mother, Babe—warned me?

My entire knowledge of how babies were made could fill an eyedropper. I blamed myself. I should have made it my business to find out more about these things, way back when I was eight or nine. I should have paid more attention to how our cat was always pregnant. But even the mention of the word "pregnant" was forbidden in our home, let alone how you got that way.

"Someday I'm going to have a litter of kittens," I can remember saying to Babe, shortly after she'd been hired on as camp cook. She had come to light our cookstove the morning our cat had given birth to another set behind the stove. Babe didn't like cats.

"Don't be stupid. Humans have humans, not kittens," she replied, setting down what I thought was an entire cord of wood.

"How do they do that?" I asked. How much more direct can you get than that? I knew how the kittens got *out*—what I didn't know was how they got *in*.

"None of your business how. Only sure way of not havin' babies is stayin' away from boys! You keep your legs together. No kissin', no nothin'! That's all you need to know."

So in one day, I had broken all the rules. Squirl had kissed me, lain on top of me, our legs entwined. Kissed me some more. Oh yes, it was obvious. I was done for.

How could the best day of my life have turned into the worst day of my life? Everything was so unfair. And I still had my father's wrath to suffer. I heard the door open and close downstairs. I pictured the conversation Babe was probably having with him. Naturally, they would send me away. Far away. Probably to someplace where the Catholics gave charity. Maybe even to my mother's family in China. In China, they killed bothersome daughters. Or, oh God, maybe they would have to marry me off to someone—some old toothless, one-legged logger or something. That would serve me right.

I heard my father's footsteps on the stairs. I wiped my face with my sheets. I didn't want him to see I'd been crying. He always made me go away when I was crying and told me not to come back until I could "discuss this without emotion."

He came into my room without knocking. He stood over my bed, glaring down at me. "I've fired Squirl, that no good half-breed," he said.

"Maybe one no-good half-breed deserves another," I boldly said up to my father. What did I have left to lose?

"None of your lip!" he said.

"Because in case you haven't noticed, that's what *I* am!"

"I said, none—"

"So when you say 'half-breed,' remember, I am what you made me. Or at least, *half*. . . ."

His eyes raged, but he just turned his back on me and stared out my window.

"I'm sending you to a convent in Spokane," he finally announced. "Should have done it after your mother died. Folks told me this was no place to raise a girl and they were right."

I glared up at him. It would have been one thing if he'd said it with regret, or even remorse. I knew better than to expect sadness or pity, but he spoke as though I was a heap of haphazard slash and he regretted not burning me off while I was green and manageable. As though he had waited too long, until I was so much tinder, flammable, ready and eager to cause damage.

My father continued quietly, icily, to describe the Spokane convent arrangements. Of course, I realized there was no way he could have arranged all this so quickly. So I knew he'd assumed I'd end up there someday anyway. Again, this some-how comforted me. After all, if I was being called a horse thief, I might as well steal the damn horse. He rambled on, but I wasn't even listening anymore. I was planning my escape. It was Sunday and the train up the mountain would be arriving around six. No matter what I did, I had to wait until dark. Of course, everyone would know me, so my escape would have to be silent, in the dark, alone.

My father finished with, "I'm sorry it has to be this way, Cordelia. I've done my best. Let's see what God can do." Ha. And him all these years saying he was an atheist. Some atheist, turning his daughter over to nuns and confession and whatever comes after that. He left my room, but I wasn't thinking about Spokane or convents or God's turn with me. I was thinking about Squirl. Wondering how he was going to get off the mountain. Probably wait for the train and ride it back down at six. Or maybe he'd already started walking. It would be like Squirl to collect his bet, pack his gear, and start walking down the tracks.

But could I travel with this bleeding? Would simple movement destroy me and my contents? Babe had told me I had to be still for several days. Yet my cat had jumped around the house right up to the day she disappeared behind the stove to get her kittens out. When Meg the mule had been with foal, she'd hauled that food cart up and down camp just like she always did.

It was probably just a lie, then. Babe wanted to keep me under her thumb, watch me, punish me until the Spokane arrangements came through. Now that I knew I wasn't dying, at least not that day, I thought I had better risk it and get moving. As soon as I got some rest, that is, feeling as though my tea was drugged. I think it was. I didn't wake until Monday afternoon and even then I thought my head was going to explode. By Tuesday, I felt better and my plans of escape came back to life.

It was far from the way I'd imagined it would happen—
my leaving Centner's Mill. I'd fantasized many exits; one
even included the use of an aeroplane. I'd imagined fanfare,
fine clothes, people on the outside waiting for me, a fond
farewell and triumphant returns. I'd planned on a father
regretting his loss, Babe losing weight grieving over my ab-
sence. I'd planned a lot of escapes over the years, but never
this one, nor for these reasons.

So I would be less than honest if I was to say I wasn't a
little excited. Being pregnant, of course, put a shroud over
things. This was never, even in my wildest, most daring
dream, a part of my escape.

But plans change. So do dreams.

11

My first concern was money. I had little need of it in Centner's Mill. Some distant relative would send me a silver dollar every Christmas. I still had all fourteen of them. Of course, my father paid me wages for my work in the mill office, but those were all kept on a time sheet, to be paid (I assumed) when I had something to buy, such as a husband. At last look, that was nearly a hundred and a quarter dollars. I would need that money.

I knew they mustn't hear my footsteps creeping about my room, from closet to dresser to the satchel on my bed. So, that Tuesday evening, I waited for Babe to busy herself in her normal clamor in the kitchen downstairs. I knew I had to work quickly and quietly. I didn't even dare imagine what my fate would be if my father was to catch me running off to God knows where, and after "that Squirl." No doubt my father would think I was better off dead than in the company of Squirl. Hmmm. Better off dead. If I left a suicide note, then my father would have no reason to come looking for me. What a grand idea! So this is what I wrote:

Father:
    I am taking the money that is rightly mine. I am leaving to do away with myself. You will never see me again. You can call the nuns and tell them I won't be coming after all.
    Your daughter,
    Cordelia

Getting to the money was going to be the hard part. But I knew the safe in the office had enough to meet a cash payroll. My father always said he had to keep that much on hand. You never knew when the entire crew would demand cash instead of company credit at the commissary, especially with all the strike rumors flying.

I pulled out four dresses and smashed them flat into my satchel. I chose ones that had liberal waistlines or large seams that I could let out as I needed. I threw in a pair of dungarees and my work boots. Not so much because I thought I might have to wear them wherever I was going, but just because they were good, sturdy wear. I took the photograph of my mother out of the silver frame and placed it on the bottom, along with paper, pencil, what was left of my meager art supplies, the pepper shaker and some stamps from my writing box. A few toiletries and I was packed. On top were the rags Babe had tossed down on my bed. I knew that having babies was a bloody affair.

All I needed now was a plan. I stashed my satchel deep inside my closet, climbed back into bed and waited for inspiration to hit.

When the house was dark, finally, for the evening, I worked up my courage to leave. Lying in my warm bed, the covers tight and secure around me, I came very close to changing my mind . . . to staying right there in that bed and facing my father and my fate. To die in that bed, death by guilt, death by shame, death by childbirth. Then I thought of having to endure Babe, my father, the whole camp, staring down at me, pointing their fingers as I was carted away, pregnant, to the convent. No. I would face any unknowns in the outside world rather than face what I knew in Centner's Mill. Making my father think the world was soon to be rid of me seemed like an inspiration. It never occurred to me that suicides usually don't take money, a satchel and four dresses with them into that Great Beyond.

I grabbed my satchel and made a quick turn around the house to make sure I was alone. Sometimes Babe would stay out on the porch overlooking the millpond and smoke a cigar—late, alone and in the dark. The last obstacle I needed was her. I doubted, in my condition, I could outrun her.

I crept into my father's library and lit his desk lamp. All I needed was the key to the mill office. I knew the safe combination. That's how little my father knew me. That's how surprised he was going to be to find that safe short my wages and my suicide note in their place. It would be the last thing my father ever would have thought of me. Well, the next to the last thing. I'm sure the last thing was my condition.

I found the key and walked to the mill as fast as I could. The chill of the mountains was settling down over the cove and I remembered I'd forgotten to pack my winter coat. Wherever I was going, winter would come. Since my satchel was full, I decided I was going to have to wear it. I paused on the steps of the mill office and looked around. The dusk was falling and, I had to admit, Centner's Mill was lovely that time of night. The frogs were beginning their chorus and I could hear the boys down in the bachelors' quarters playing their evening concert—guitar, banjo, mandolin. Fun sounds, sounds of life and high spirits and good news and longtime friends.

There was no one on the street to see me sneak in, open the safe and count out my wages. In the place of one hundred twenty-five dollars, I made a note in the payroll ledger I was paid in full. The entry before mine was the one my father had last entered: "Squirl, Final Time and Wages: $37.50." I closed the safe and sneaked back out. This time, I stashed my satchel in the bushes outside the office while I quickly went back up the hill to return the key to my father's desk. I got my coat and a Thermos bottle full of water from the kitchen and took a handful of rock candy from the bowl on the piano. I did a quick inventory of what I had packed. I'd forgotten Gert, my favorite childhood doll. Poor Gert. She'd never forgive me if I didn't take her. All the times she and I had planned on seeing the world together . . .

In my room, looking around for the last time, with Gert under my arm and my coat over my shoulders, I said goodbye and good luck to the walls, the ceiling, the rag rug on the floor. I closed the door quickly and tiptoed down the hall.

Why I lingered so, I don't know. It was now or never. I went to the parlor and sat down in Babe's huge, special-made chair. I must have looked like a white china doll myself, lost in the arms of the chair, my legs sticking straight out.

I looked over at the baby grand piano, remembering the day it had arrived. I'd been thrilled, thinking we'd at last have music in the house. I was dead wrong. Babe just scowled down at me, said it wasn't the piano at all she wanted. She only wanted the box it came in, which was beautifully crafted and had small rows of dainty flowers stenciled along the top. Babe told me she'd ordered this brand of piano because she'd heard the boxes were a work of art. She kept it in the barn, safely preserved in oily tarps, and she'd threatened my life if I ever went *near* it. "Least now I know I got me a respectable coffin, comes my time," she added. "Comes my time" couldn't come soon enough for me, I was thinking.

The memory of that snapped me back to my senses. It had come *my* time. I popped out of the chair and left for good.

Dusk was done. It was now totally black out. I had only the rising moon to light my way. But the rising moon and maybe a few bright stars were all I needed—remember, I preferred the darkness. My eyes never hurt in the dark. Some people even thought I had cat eyes, that I could see better in the dark than in the day. I let them believe it because in a way, I did too.

Since I was now a runaway, maybe even a thief, a "girl in trouble" and God knows what else, I would need my night skills. The moon, the stars and gaslight were now my allies.

But Squirl. Where was he? How could he possibly know the tragedy that had befallen us? How does one tell someone news like I had? Would he do his duty by me and take me away, save me, marry me and be with me forever?

Men got girls "in trouble." That I knew from the gossip I now and then overheard while waiting for the mail, or sitting on the bench in front of the mercantile or helping out in the dinner hall. Decent men "did right by 'em." "Do right" meant take care of. Take care of meant take away, love, hide, protect.

So all I knew was I had to find Squirl. And there was only one place Squirl would go—Seattle. It may as well have been a flame and Squirl a moth, by the way he talked about Seattle, Luna Park, Cousin Sally.

I'd envied him so much as he'd talked about Seattle. How wonderful to always have a place, no matter where you ever went, no matter what you ever did, to go home to. "To go home to"—what four wonderful, comforting words those were. Centner's Mill and those words would never share any sentence I would ever utter. But Seattle—that was where Squirl would go, especially since he had at least $37.50 plus his bet winnings. He'd probably climb down out of the hills, pick up the Northern Pacific toward Olympia and from there go north to Tacoma, then on to Seattle. After all, he wasn't leaving in a cloak of shame like I was. Why should he care who saw him?

But I couldn't risk anyone seeing me sneak down off our mountain. I wasn't about to leave a trail. Not that I thought my father would come after me, unless perhaps just to have the last word—to be obeyed all the way to that convent in Spokane. I was good riddance. But leaving a trail would have been just plain stupid.

It also would have been just plain stupid of me to think I could walk down off the mountain. Even under the best of circumstances—like in the daylight with nothing to carry and not pregnant—it was a dangerous journey. Everyone took the train. Then it hit me! My second inspiration since the suicide note. We had several portable bunkhouses lined up to be hauled back down the mountain. Hide in one of those, Cordy! I thought. Perfect! More than perfect—sheer genius! A bunk car would be warm, protected, maybe even cozy. I might be able to hopscotch my way clear to Seattle, or at least Aberdeen, and it wouldn't cost me a dime!

So I worked my way down to the depot, which was little more than some small warehouses, a couple of benches and a platform of decking along both sides of the track. I stayed out of the moonlight as best I could. A warm breeze was coming up the small canyon that embraced the tracks and I was sorry I'd dressed so warmly.

I could make out the bunkhouse cars because they were painted white, as though to make them look more like sweet little country homes. I counted six of them on a small spur of track, all strung together waiting for their turn out of town. I climbed the steps of the last car, cupped my hands around the window in the door and looked in. Although it was dark, I could make out some niceties. This car had Priscilla curtains, a tablecloth and even a bedspread on the bunk. This car must have belonged to a married logger, for no bachelor lumberman would ever have stood for such a lovely bunkhouse.

I tried the door. Naturally, it was locked. Then I heard footsteps on the crunchy cinder bed along the tracks. I sat down and plastered myself against the steps. I listened, holding my breath. I could hear the jingling of keys and I knew it was Archie, the night watchman for the mill. He had a habit of constantly playing with his key chain. You could hear him coming for a country mile. But my father insisted that Archie was good at his job, even if his keys did announce his arrival. Could it be they had already noticed I was gone and had sent him looking?

Well, *that* was dumb, I thought as I heard Archie unlock the office door, go inside, then close the door behind him. I crept down off the steps, peeked around the bunkhouse car, and watched my father's crackerjack night watchman cradle his head in his arms for a nap.

But Archie had served a purpose for me that night. I realized I was too close to home to hide. They would find me missing by seven in the morning, I figured—no later. If, stabbed by guilt, they did decide to look for me, no doubt this depot, maybe even this car, was where they would come looking. Well, all they would find would be Archie, all refreshed and ready to help in the search.

I picked up my satchel, put my coat over my shoulders and started walking down the tracks. I'd been down the mountain as far as Cosmopolis—probably fifteen miles away—and I knew that the train stopped at three other small communities along the way. I would do this: walk down the tracks until I either could go no more and fell over dead, or made it to Brooklyn, the next settlement downstream.

I started down the tracks. I don't know when exactly I started to cry—maybe I'd been crying the whole way. I just didn't notice it until my eyes began to smart, which they seldom did in the dark. How, I asked myself, had the simple task of leaving become so difficult? For all the times I'd planned my escape—for all the days I'd numbered on all my calendars, counting down to that final glorious day of freedom—you'd think I would have had things better in hand. Of course, being pregnant confused everything.

I was doing everything for two now—thinking, plotting, escaping, crying.

12

The track followed the North River down to Brooklyn. I saw only one light welcoming my arrival. Exhausted, I put my satchel down, leaned up against it, and wondered what I should do next. I looked back up the mountain. In and out of a swaying breeze, I could see the faint glow of a few lights—that would be Centner's Mill. One of the faint lights might even have been coming from my own home, my own room.

I looked back down to the one light below in Brooklyn. Brooklyn, I thought. What deluded logger came up with that name? Brooklyn—here in the middle of the mountains. The Brooklyn everyone'd heard of was in New York City. This Brooklyn was Brooklyn as in "brook"—the small rivulet that ran off the North River and powered a now-extinct sawmill.

It was there, leaning against my carpetbag satchel, that I fell asleep. I didn't wake until the earth moved under me the next morning. The train was coming down the mountain. That was the rumbling I felt under me. I dashed into the woods and waited for the small lokie engine to peek around the bend. I imagined men in each car hanging out the windows, looking for me and calling my name. "Cordelia, come home! All is forgiven!" Surely they must have noticed I was gone by now. Found my note, maybe. Would they be combing the hills? Dragging the pond? Ask the doc if I'd been in for a dose of cyanide?

The train rumbled forward, its two speeds being slow and crawling. No one looked out the windows or called my name. I watched the engine go by. The driver—who was that? Looked like Hank Healy. Hard to tell with his nose buried in a newspaper.

Several of the bunk cars were chugging along and I waited for the front of the train to go around the Brooklyn bend before I crept out of the woods. Without the platform, the steps were high but not impossible, even for my short legs. I waited for the last one to come along, tossed my satchel and coat onto the stairs, then grabbed the handles, walked along a few paces, jumped, dangled monkeylike, my skirts almost smothering me, and pulled myself up.

I waited for the train to begin the small grade up before the gentle glide back down and into Brooklyn. That's when the groan of the small engine was the loudest and no one would hear me smash the window in the door. I was grateful I had taken my heavy coat, because I wrapped my hand in it to break the window. The rest was fast and easy. Open the door, knock out the remnants of glass to make it look untouched from a distance and tack down the curtains.

I hid my gear under the bunk. I secured the windows along the backside of my car and I practiced fitting into the slim closet, which would be my hiding place when we were in a station. Now *this* was more like it. Escape in style, Priscilla curtains and all.

Brooklyn was easy. No one came looking. Nor did they at Vesta or Arctic, hamlets farther down the line. By the time we were approaching Cosmopolis, I was a lot more relaxed. I no longer hid in the closet as the train chugged into civilization. In fact, I sat at the window, carefully peeking out of the curtains, planning my next step.

I tried to imagine how Squirl would get himself to Seattle. I looked out over Grays Harbor as the train crossed it, imagined the Pacific Ocean beyond and realized he could very well hop a steamer, ride the rail or even fly to Seattle from Aberdeen. Fly? Yes, I'd seen aeroplanes. My father's company had even hired them to survey new logging sections. We'd see barnstormers, too, gliding by on their way to the coast once in a while. You'd hear the faraway buzz—no sound like it. The sound of an approaching aeroplane would bring all work to a halt. Everyone would come out to look. I knew there was an aeroplane in Aberdeen. Was I really thinking about finding it? Did I have the courage? Flying to Seattle would be the one way of getting there my father would never suspect of me.

Flying would be the fastest way too. Could I afford it? Could I risk it? Would the pilot even take me? I was such an odd little runaway. What would be my reason? Would he know me as that little albino daughter of Red Hankins's? That's the major problem with being one of a kind. Few people forget me.

This was going to take some planning, some lying, maybe some disguising. But if I was going to survive outside of Centner's Mill at all, for even a day, I would need to learn these skills and many, many more.

I may have entered that bunk car a fourteen-year-old half-Chinese albino in trouble, but I was far from that as I carefully jumped out of the car in Aberdeen. I was now a little old lady, in black from head to toe to fingertips, with dark glasses and a broom-handle cane. Blind.

It was the third of July and Aberdeen was laid out in red, white and blue bunting, making me almost a black blind ghost strolling among the gaiety.

People were more than anxious to help this poor blind wayfarer to find her way to a milliner's shop. There I bought a proper black hat with a long, dark veil. This completed my widow's weeds. The veil offered me the perfect disguise. I could see out and no one could see in. The old blind lady was now just another young widow in mourning. With the war, with the influenza, we were everywhere . . . all ages, all sizes, all destinations.

From there I went to the funeral parlor, where I bought an urn. That was easy. The man was more than happy to sell me one. He acted like it was one of a kind, but we both knew he'd pull out another one just like it from the storeroom after I'd left.

Either the town of Aberdeen was incredibly stupid or else I was amazingly smart. No one even gave me a suspicious glance. It didn't occur to me that no one cared who I was or what I was doing. The truth of the matter was, I was the stupid one. I'd never been in a town that size. That day was the first time I had used a public telephone, hired a taxicab, walked down a street where I didn't know a soul or been helped across the street by a man in a uniform.

I was a quick learner, especially when I had an aeroplane to catch. The pilot had agreed by telephone to fly me and my urn of ashes (which was really just sand from the railroad bed) to Seattle. There, over Puget Sound, I would toss them out. He said I was lucky because he had a flying show up in the Seattle area the very next day, Independence Day. The fact that he was going anyway made no difference in what I would have to pay. Thirty dollars. In advance.

The pilot was very kind to this young widow. He stowed my gear in a hatch in front of where I was to sit. I wouldn't let him take the urn from me. Nice, grief-filled touch, I thought. But dumb, because that only left me one free hand to use to pull myself up on the wing and then into the passenger's seat. The urn dropped to the ground. All I needed was for the contents to spill out and the pilot to see the red cinders and dirty, rocky sand from the railroad bed, rather than the fine silt of Charles Greeley, the name I had chosen for my poor departed husband.

We looked at each other, then down to the urn. He picked it up and carefully handed it to me with his heartfelt apologies. Thank God for my veil or else he'd have known I was closer to laughter than to tears.

I held the urn in my lap and wound the long black scarf from my widow's *chapeau* around my head to keep it secure. The pilot swung the propeller around a few times with mighty swings, then, when it took, climbed into his cockpit, right behind me. I'd be lying if I said I wasn't scared. And of course, I was excited as the plane took off. But I was comparing it to the exhilaration I'd felt holding on to Squirl as we sped down the flume. No matter what I would ever do in life, I was certain that sharing that log raft with Squirl was going to be the pinnacle. What I was doing now, anything I would ever do, was nothing but leftovers.

When I dared to look down all I could see was dense fog. But the fog soon began to lift as we went inland. We followed a river toward the east and I looked eagerly at the northern horizon for Seattle. I imagined the city would simply burst out of the emerald green of the never-ending forests and glisten in the sun somewhere just ahead. But all around us, all I could see were the forests, dotted here and there with clear-cuts, sometimes a pasture, sometimes a cow or a horse, but mostly just the forests. For the first two hours, only never-ending green. I imagined somewhere below, there were logging trails, railroad tracks; maybe even Squirl was down there, making his own way to Seattle. Was he looking up, shading his eyes against the sun, seeing this plane and me in it at this very moment?

Then it happened. The pilot tapped on the plane just behind me, calling my attention to the northern horizon. I nearly forgot I was a mourning widow and lifted my veil and my glasses to get a better glimpse of the shiny specks of silver, gray and white poking into the sky. Oh my God, I *had* sketched Seattle that day on the hillside. For as we got closer there was—what had Squirl called it? The Smith Building? A short moment later and we could see a forest of masts from what must have been hundreds of sailing ships in the bay. Closer still and I could see the other buildings, climbing hills; houses, thousands of them everywhere! Streets! Automobiles! As we flew over the city, I could barely keep my breath steady. I looked down and could see the shadows of the city canyons. And the part I couldn't make out, the life, the excitement as people rushed about their wonderful city lives, I swear I could feel from high above.

Then I saw it. The Luna Park that Squirl had told me about. It had to be. The jumble of narrow-gauge track was a roller coaster and that big round thing a Ferris wheel. And what was that? A huge glass building, domed at the top and reflecting our very image as we flew over it. From above, the park seemed to be a whole other small town—streets, walkways, trains, nestled on the waterfront and bigger than life.

The pilot took us out over the water again and I could see the islands in Puget Sound and the water trails the boats were leaving. He signaled down below and at first I thought he was just pointing something out to me. I looked over the edge of the biplane and saw nothing that should have impressed me more than anything else. I looked at him again and he was making a motion as though he was throwing something overboard. Then I remembered. I wasn't a runaway, joyriding through the sky to find her love. I was a grieving widow, waiting to cast my husband's ashes into Puget Sound as I had been instructed by his Last Will and Testament.

I'd grown rather fond of the urn. It had given me a certain sense of security—a weight of authority on my lap, holding me down in case my widow's weeds became airborne and me along with them. I sort of hated to let it go. But the pilot was banging on the plane and I decided, since that was what I had hired him to do, I should get on with it.

I threw the urn overboard and watched it fall. The moment I did I could hear the pilot screaming from his cockpit behind me. I could hear his "Oh God, noooooooooo!" clear over the drone of the engine.

What was wrong? I looked back down and saw the urn crash into the rigging of a sailing vessel below. The plane took a quick turn up and to the right, and although I didn't think we could go much faster, it seemed we were now, well, running away. The men on the ship below were running toward the mast, which had several spars broken and rigging flapping in the breeze.

When we landed at the strip just east of Seattle, a place called Sand Point, the pilot tapped me on the shoulder, lifted his goggles, and said, "Mrs. Greeley, you was *supposed* to send over just the ashes, not the whole urn." He gave me a stern lecture and told me that if those sailors had got the name of his plane he was done for. Then he apologized for yelling at me in my grief, for I made an effort to find a hankie in my satchel.

He helped me out of the aeroplane and said he'd call a taxicab to come and collect me. He asked me if I'd like to sit in the shade while I waited. I nodded bravely and allowed him to help me to a small building along the landing strip. I'd read that most widows were supposed to be tightfisted with their usually slim inheritances, so I played the role to the fullest. I opened my little beaded bag, which was attached to my belt, reached in and gave the pilot a dime and thanked him for everything. He tried to give it back, which I thought was rather funny, since he'd been so remorseless in keeping to his flying price of thirty dollars. But I was learning about the ways of the world and this was one of them.

Earning is one thing, taking is another.

I took back the dime and said goodbye and thank you once again and that I hoped no one was hurt on that sailing ship back in the harbor. My widowhood had gotten me this far—no questions asked. In fact, widowhood had been very good to me. I decided to remain a widow until I was situated in Seattle.

Maybe even until the baby came.

13

"Where will it be, ma'am?" the taxi driver asked, tipping his cap and picking up my satchel.

Where to indeed? I thought, standing up. I simply stated all I knew: "Luna."

"Luna?" he asked back. "You mean Looney Park? You want to go to Looney Park?"

"No, I want to go to Luna Park," I corrected him. I saw nothing looney at all about my request.

"You sure, ma'am?" the driver asked back. He turned and looked at the aeroplane, still on the field, then back at me. "Kinda strange, a lady like you wanting to go to a place like that. I mean, you fly into town like you own the place just to go to a trashy joint like Looney Park?" I couldn't tell if he was talking to me or my satchel as he stowed it for me. Already I could see how different people were in the city and already I was adapting.

"But I have to," I insisted.

"Don't seem right," he muttered.

I said sadly, "I have to fulfill my husband's last wish." I dabbed my eyes, under my veil, with my hankie.

He looked at me; then a big smile spread across his face. He said, "The roller coaster, right?"

Sure, I thought, if it'll get me there. I nodded dramatically, my veil shivering as I did. "How did you know?"

He climbed in the car and said, "Lots of you war widders coming to Seattle for last wishes. But don't you wanna, I mean, don't you have—"

"Money? I have money," I interrupted, ready to show him.

He looked at me over his shoulder and said, "Ain't that, ma'am. Don't you want I should take you to some relatives or friends first? Maybe a nice hotel?"

"No. Luna Park, please."

"My missus'd skin me alive if she knew I'd taken a nice widder woman like you and left you there. Hardly any decent places to stay, even."

I looked at the driver as directly as my veil would let me. "Have you ever been in an aeroplane?"

"Well, no."

"It's not a very pleasant experience. I would even say I risked my very life in that contraption. But I did it. Do you know why?"

"Last wishes?"

It was working. I nodded and he said, "Luna Park it is."

We drove for what seemed like an hour—what took the aeroplane only minutes took the car forever. Slowly the countryside melted into areas of small homes, a few sawmills and pulp mills, and finally I could see the Smith Building off in the distance. I was really there. Seattle.

We rumbled down a road and I wondered why a town this

size, this magnificent, didn't have better streets. Even the main road in Centner's Mill was smoother than the one we were bumping down. I feared for my condition and wondered if this would cause my bleeding to come back. One rut was so deep that I could hear the bottom of the automobile scrape beneath me. The driver did his best to keep his curses civil. Had he only known my upbringing—that lumberman language was tougher than sailor language. Taximan language wasn't even in the running.

The closer we got to the city, the more traffic swooshed by us. I had never imagined so many automobiles in one place, all moving so fast together. There was a man, some sort of constable, standing in the middle of the street, and he'd simply hold up a hand, blow a whistle, and cars would stop or come on through as he directed. Even the horses obeyed his signals. At first I thought he must be crazy, then I thought he was probably very brave, too.

And the noises! I don't know where the noises were coming from, because they just seemed to echo down through the streets. Car horns, those I knew, because my own taxi driver tooted his horn at every opportunity. But there was a general din of unknown origins—just city sounds, I supposed.

And oh, the people! How could there be so many people living, breathing, eating all in the same place? How wonderful, how exciting, and yet how strange for me to be there, seeing Seattle through the layers of my veil and not yet knowing where I was going, what I was doing or whom I should be fearing.

"So, where you from?" the taximan asked, giving me a casual look over his shoulder.

Careful now, I told myself. "Oh, down south," I replied.

"How far south?"

"A . . . A small town down Olympia way." Pretty nosy, I thought.

"How's the influenza down that way?"

Naturally, I knew perfectly well about the influenza, although no one was stricken yet up in Centner's Mill. "Oh, about the same as everywhere," I said, thinking that was probably true.

"That what made you a widder?" he asked.

"Um, no," I replied, reminding myself to mourn more and *oooh* and *ahh* over the sights less. "The war."

"Ah. Sorry, ma'am. France?"

France? You mean now I had to come up with where my supposed husband had died? Okay, France it was.

I wanted off that subject, so I asked him, "Lots of the flu here in Seattle?"

"They're droppin' like flies," he said. Then he looked back around at me and added, "Say, you folks from smaller towns gotta be careful here in the city, you know. My missus says you folks from small towns don't got . . . what's she call it . . . don't got good immunity! That's it. Immunity. So you might keep that veil on when you're in big public places. Don't go breathing more'n you have to." Then he laughed and added, "I mean, you know what I mean."

We finally came to the waterfront, alive with commerce, people and more fascinating sights than I had ever imagined. Then we approached what I'd have to call a plank road—a wood road, almost like you'd see in the mountains, only instead of skidding logs down this plank road, the man drove his taxi down it.

At first I thought he'd taken a wrong turn, for this road

was built out over the water—a long, low bridge crossing the corner of Puget Sound.

We thunked along for some time, slowing to move over when another car came at us. The sun was beginning to get low over the Olympic Mountains on the western horizon. When we hit land again the wonders of Luna Park began to appear before us.

He said since it was getting late, maybe I should find me a nice cabin, well kept and respectable, where I could spend the night, and would I please allow him to find me a place?

"No, I want to go to Cousin Sally's," I stated.

He gave me that over-the-shoulder look that I was now getting used to. He pulled the taxi over, stopped and turned to face me full.

"Ma'am, I couldn't go home and face my ol' lady if I told her I took a nice widder woman like you to Cousin Sally's," he said, echoing his previous objections.

"You know Cousin Sally?" I asked.

"Well, no," he began, "but I've hauled plenty of drunks home from that cab joint. Nope, can't take you there. Not Cousin Sally's."

"But a friend said that's *the* place," I said, recalling Squirl's snapping eyes when he'd said those very same words.

"Then I think your friend's playing a joke on you. Fine thing and in your current state, I might add."

Oh God, he could tell just by looking at me that I was pregnant! Then he added as he pulled back onto the road, "I mean, you being in mourning and all."

I gave a small sigh of relief. "But I have to meet some-one . . ."

"Look, lady, why don't we find you a telephone and you

can make a call to your family? Bad enough you wanting to go to Looney Park, and unescorted and all. But Cousin Sally's . . . No, I just can't allow . . ."

"Will it make you feel better if we find one of those nice cabins? You've been so kind, I don't want you to get in trouble with your wife," I said. I hadn't come this far just to be held back by the wishes of some taxi driver's wife. I masked the disappointment in my voice.

Clean, safe, cheap—why not? I thought. Then tomorrow, after a good rest, I would begin my search for Squirl.

We pulled up to a nice, homey-looking building called the West Inn Housekeeping Cabins. He stopped, helped me out of the car and got out my satchel. I paid him all he asked and, like the aeroplane man, he accepted no tip.

"So, you be careful, ma'am," he said. "Seattle can be a rough place." He tipped his hat and left at last.

I walked up the steps, entered the main part of the inn and waited for someone to answer the bell at the front desk. I looked at my reflection in the mirror behind the desk and realized I wasn't anything I had appeared to be that day. I really was just a fourteen-year-old runaway, about to begin the most important journey of her life.

14

I registered at the West Inn under another name. Even though I'd left Centner's Mill with the log pond full, a backlog of timber high up to be sluiced down, a whole in-bin full of U.S. Department of the Navy orders for ships' decking and a suicide note, my father's conscience might force him to put an ad in the lost-and-found section of some paper. I doubted it, but just in case, I signed the guest register as Mrs. Ophelia Greeley. I figured Ophelia was about as close to Cordelia as I could get and therefore, I might not sit like an idiot while someone right next to me was saying my name. I had to endure a short interview by Mrs. Pomfert, the owner. She was very curious—maybe even suspicious.

Being a war widow had gotten me this far, so I was not going to change horses now. And lying is easier when dark glasses and a veil are between you and the questions.

I was shown my cabin. It was right on the boardwalk and looked out over the Seattle skyline and the waterfront. I could see the masts from the ships in the bay, the smoke from stacks of industry to the south and the tall green spires of trees to the north. I had a bed, a table, a sitting chair, a fireplace, a small kitchen and a private bath that I had to pay extra for. Here's something: I had a buzzer, which Mrs. Pomfert told me would buzz once if there was mail, twice if there was a phone call and three times if there was a visitor. I had to push a button to buzz back and let them know I'd gotten the message. I knew if that buzzer went off for anything, I'd be packed and out my window in minutes.

I slept like a baby that night. I fell to sleep reliving my escape—I'd gotten this far using brains and charm, two things Babe always said I lacked. I'd been a stowaway, a blind woman, a bereaved widow, an aeroplane bombardier, a taxicab rider, and now I was Mrs. Ophelia Greeley. I was beginning to like this.

I fell asleep thinking: Tomorrow, Squirl.

The next morning, the Fourth of July, the waterfront seemed to beckon to me as surely as it had beckoned to Squirl from Centner's Mill. I couldn't bear to be a widow that first Seattle morning. It was early, just after dawn, so I simply tied a scarf on my head and put on a dull sweater. The heavy fog that I had always heard about didn't disappoint me. It was cool and wonderful on my face. It was so gray in the early morning that I even dared to walk without my glasses on my nose but left them dangling from the string around my neck. I kept my glance low. No use alarming passersby or startling horses on this glorious, foggy Independence Day morning.

I went along the boardwalk and stood, I don't know for how long, just watching the water lap up along the beach. What a wonderful sound! As regular and as expected as a heartbeat. I could hardly keep from being mesmerized by the rhythm. If the shore of Puget Sound was this grand, I didn't dare imagine what the Pacific Ocean beyond those mountains must be like. I vowed to see it as soon as I could.

There was ferryboat traffic scooting here and there, masts of ships from far away coming or going, seagulls darting, canoes, rowboats—such activity, I hardly knew where to look. And this was only the beach—Luna Park was still two blocks away.

Vowing to savor every moment, inhale every sight, sound and smell, I took my time along my walk. The closer I got to the park, the more excitement I felt in the air. A large boatload of people had just arrived and they were all walking up the gangway—gaily laughing, carrying baskets, looking bright and rich and lovely. What bliss to be so carefree.

I ducked into the shade of a shed and just watched as they walked by. The dresses! Not nearly as long here in Seattle—I saw ankles and lovely, narrow, dainty shoes. Even the men looked heavenly in all the shades of white and cream and beige. Of course, I knew my days of wearing white were now over, but I admired it so on the ladies passing by. Who were these people? What did they do in the city? What homes did they return to?

I let the crowd pass by before I ventured out of the shade. Then I put my glasses back on so I could stare at people as they passed. That's one of the advantages of having to wear smoked glasses—you can stare at things and no one is the wiser, unless you're practically nose-to-nose. I wondered if anyone even noticed me when there were so many other things to look at.

I loved it. So much so that I'd briefly forgotten my mission: Squirl. "Cousin Sally of Luna Park" were his exact words. Then I remembered the taxi driver's reaction to

Cousin Sally's. I hate to admit it, but I wasn't scared off. I was—in a way—excited to see for myself.

I spied a friendly-looking woman, a street vendor I thought, coming my way up the boardwalk. She carried a large net bag, which had several fish tails sticking out. Two cats were at her heels, and I could tell by the way she was trying not to really kick them as she walked that she liked cats. She just didn't want to trip over them, and so I thought this woman would be the one to ask.

"Pardon me, ma'am," I said. "Do you know where I could find Cousin Sally's?"

The fish woman batted absently at the cats at her feet. "Got me a friend who had a Aunt Sally, but nope . . . Wait a minute. You don't want to know where *Cousin* Sally's is, do you?"

Somehow, if you emphasize the "Cousin" portion, you get a whole other person. I nodded.

"What's a girl the likes of you want with a place the likes of Cousin Sally's?"

I noticed one of the cats was tasting a fish fin through the net bag, but the woman was so concerned about me, I think that cat could have jumped in that bag, eaten the entire fish and burped loudly and she wouldn't have noticed.

I made something up—delivering an important message, I think.

The woman gave me a look of disapproval, then changed it to pity when she looked more closely at me. But she gave me directions anyway—down this boardwalk, turn right, minding the streetcar crossing, then there on the corner—if I missed it I was blind. "And good luck to you, honey!" she called out after me.

So, down the boardwalk, right turn and yes, the streetcars

ran fast. I wasn't blind, for there it was, larger than life and sporting an electric lightbulb sign:

Cousin Sally's

Then, painted in large, elegant lettering:

Entertainment for Gentlemen
Billiards, Refreshments, Overnight Accommodations

It was the most ornate, beautiful building I had ever seen. Gold around the doors and windows, bright red lettering, huge gas torches protecting a canvas-covered walkway, and a man in a red and gold uniform standing like a guard in front.

Naturally, I'd heard of Negroes before, but that man in his dazzling uniform was the first I had ever seen anywhere. My father never would have hired even a Mexican, let alone a black man.

Finally the man came over to me and said in a voice as low as a gurgling boiler, "Go away."

My first instinct was to *run* away. But I remembered my precious Squirl and my condition and my mission.

"I need to see Cousin Sally."

He laughed so loud I thought the canvas over our heads would come crashing down. I could see inside his mouth—his teeth were as large and as white as piano keys, laced with gold—yes, gold!

"Why is that so funny?" I found the nerve to ask.

"My dear," he said, "do you know what time it is?"

I pulled out my watch from my pocket and informed him it was just now eight-thirty.

"In the morning, dear," he said.

"Yes. So?"

"Cousin Sally ain't even gone to bed yet."

"Then why can't I see her?" I asked. What did I care if the woman was a night owl? I'd stayed up plenty of times all night reading.

"She don't see no one at eight-thirty A.M. in the morning," he further informed me. "Even her banker."

"Well," I countered, pulling a pencil out of my skirt pocket. "Could you give her a note?"

"This business?" he asked, folding his arms in front of him.

"Uh, no, personal," I said. "I'm looking for a friend and she might know where he is."

There was a buzz from a box by the door and a voice came out of it. The voice was fuzzy, but the guard went over and spoke back into it. Ignoring me, he snapped his fingers and, as though it had been waiting for him, a taxicab pulled up to the door. Then the grand golden door of the building opened and out came a man, dressed like—well, like nothing I had ever seen, but I was getting used to that. As a cover-to-cover reader of the Sears, Roebuck catalog, I knew these were what they called formal togs—a suit you wore to see an opera or a ballet or maybe were buried in, for all I knew.

He whisked by me and the guard opened the car door for him and he was gone—just like that—as quickly and as grandly as he had appeared.

I finished my note and handed it to the guard. To my surprise, he read it, then looked back down at me as though *he* would decide whether or not to take it to Cousin Sally based on my spelling and punctuation.

"Wait here," he ordered. Then, sizing me up, he added,

"On second thought, wait here." And he pulled me close to the building and had me stand next to a column, I suppose to hide me.

He went inside and the ten minutes he was gone must have been the longest in my life.

15

Standing alone, hidden by a pillar, I went over what I had written on my note.

My dear Cousin Sally,
     It's most important I speak to you regarding the matter of locating a mutual friend.
     Thank you.

I tried to make my horrible handwriting as elegant and as adult as I could, but when it came to the signature, I really scribbled it. Even I couldn't read it. I knew scribbled signatures appear far more important than ones you can read. Like my father's. I defy you to find Red Hankins anywhere in his signature.

The buzzer from the little brass box next to the door sounded. I looked at it. It buzzed again and I carefully approached it. I touched the button back and the fuzzy sound of the guard's voice came through it. I nearly jumped a foot.

I pushed the button again and he repeated his message: "When the door buzzes, open it."

I opened the heavy door and eased my way inside. I had to stand for a moment to adjust my eyes to the dark. I hated meeting people for the first time in a room so dark I couldn't use my smoked glasses.

I was in a large lobby, very similar to a hotel lobby I'd seen on a postcard someone sent my father. The floor was gray and white marble. There must have been acres of burgundy-colored velvet curtains falling from the double-high ceiling to the floor. Huge golden mirrors hung on the walls. And from the ceiling hung chandeliers of such magnificence I knew I'd sacrifice my eyes to see them all lit up and glowing. There was a curved staircase of the most beautifully carved mahogany I'd ever seen.

My eyes had adjusted and I kept my glasses on. I seemed to be alone in the huge room. From somewhere high above I could hear the faint sounds of music. Then from above me I heard a click of something mechanical and I looked up. A small golden cage was slowly moving down toward me. I stepped back and watched it come to rest on the wall in front of me. Then, as though the cage was alive and saw me standing there, its doors opened, inviting me into its tiny parlor with two red velvet stools. I crept forward, carefully stepped into the cage and sat upon a stool. The cage doors closed and locked and I heard another click from above. The cage started to move up.

Yes, I knew it was an elevator. No, I didn't know they could operate all by themselves. It carried me slowly up three stories. No sooner had the elevator stopped, than another cage door opened behind me.

I stood up and began to get frightened. I knew I was far

from my own element—this huge place, the gilded cage climbing the wall—what was I doing? Whoever this Cousin Sally was, why couldn't she just come down to greet me like a normal person?

Again I entered a room like none I had ever seen. It was full of brocade fabrics, gold, silver and crystal ornaments, strange, colorful carpets, portraits, mirrors. And on a couch across the room sat a woman. Now, if someone were to ask me to imagine what a woman would wear, sitting in a room like that, I would have said she'd be dressed in furs, laces, flourishes and feathers. But this woman wore—now, I want to get this right, so you get the full effect—she wore a man's suit of woolen gray stripes and a man's shirt, except the collar was off, and it was open at the neck. Her tie was of shiny red satin and it just hung about her neck. She had pink slippers on her feet and her hair was done all up and was held together by combs, which glittered under the soft light.

"And what do we have here?" she asked, her voice warm and wonderful. She held her hand out to me.

I came forward a few steps. There was no doubt I was, at that moment, the ugliest thing ever to have disgraced that room.

I didn't know women could shake hands when they met like men did. I came forward, took hers—which was maybe the softest hand I had ever touched—and announced myself by name.

"Cordelia Hankins," I said, totally forgetting about my alias.

"Sally Littlehook Burleson," she said back.

"*Cousin* Sally?" I asked.

She smiled and I was immediately envious of her large

white teeth, her olive skin and dark hair. We always envy what we know we can never have.

"I'm sure I'm someone's cousin," she answered. Then she rang a tiny crystal bell and a maid appeared. I knew she was a maid by the uniform she wore. She came in carrying a huge silver tray with coffee and small cakes.

"Oh, thank you, Gina, I thought you'd forgotten," Cousin Sally said.

I was asked to sit and have coffee and something to eat.

While she poured the coffee, Gina the maid looked at me with great curiosity. She placed the coffee on the table next to me and told me it was at three o'clock with a cake at four. I looked at her like she was crazy. She touched my hand and explained, "My brother's blind."

"Oh, I'm not blind," I said, embarrassed, touching my glasses. "I just have—sensitive eyes."

Gina left and I smiled weakly at Cousin Sally. I caught her glancing at a large clock on the fireplace mantel.

"So why is it you've come to see me?"

She was so beautiful, I could barely keep my eyes off of her. I knew all about makeup—lip, cheek and eye paint. But I think this was the first time I'd ever seen it applied to a face. It fascinated me.

"A . . . A friend said, if ever I got to Seattle, to look you up."

"I'm sorry, dear, I'm not hiring."

"Oh, I wasn't looking for work. You see, you see, I was looking for my friend." My words trailed off. What would a river rat like Squirl have to do with an elegant place like this? I realized how silly my quest must have sounded.

"And who is this friend of yours?" she asked.

"All I know is his nickname. Look, I think I must have the wrong Cousin Sally," I added, setting down my coffee cup.

"What's your friend's name?"

"Well," I said, feeling like there was nothing much to lose, "all I know him by is Squirl."

Instead of laughing, she sat back, smiled, nodded and said, "You have the right Cousin Sally."

I guess it's because I was frightened and so far away from all I'd ever known that I wasn't thinking very clearly. There was something in Cousin Sally's smile—a crookedness in the jaw perhaps. Or was it the dancing glint in her eyes? Or the glow of her skin?

"Is Squirl your son?" I blurted out.

Cousin Sally fixed me with a look that I don't think I'd ever seen before. "Just how old do you think I am?" she asked.

"Thirty-five?" I ventured.

At this, Cousin Sally stood up. She was much taller than I'd imagined. Maybe it was the trousers and the high-heeled slippers that made her look so tall. Anyway, she walked to a table, put a cigarette in her painted mouth, lit it and then replied, "My dear, Squirl is seventeen. I am twenty-seven. Squirl—God, I hate that nickname—is my brother. Half brother at that. Half-witted half brother too, sometimes. So, let me think: If Squirl sent you to see me that means he must have gotten you in trouble. Am I right?"

"Well, he didn't exactly send me," I said weakly. She'd seemed to be friendly at first, but now she just looked at me coolly, blowing the cigarette smoke out over my head.

"Then let me guess again," she interrupted. "Squirl told you to go see Cousin Sally and she'll put you to work. Find you a job in her fabulous palace of distractions."

"Squirl never said I could work—"

"Well, which is it? Every girl that Squirl has ever sent my way is either in trouble already or aching to soon be there."

"Trouble?" I asked.

"Let me put it to you this way: Did Squirl get you in a . . . family way?" she asked.

By the way she put it, by the wryness of her smile, all I could see was a long line of women, all pregnant and sent here by my beloved Squirl, and me at the end of the line. I couldn't help it. I burst into tears. She let me cry, which was far more than Babe would have done. I finally got control of myself and asked, "Is he here? Can I see him?"

"I don't think it's Squirl you need to be seeing," she said, her voice now a little softer.

"Oh yes!" I blubbered. "I have to see him!"

She came over and sat down next to me. She smelled of something sweet and foreign. I'd seen Paris perfumes advertised and I imagined one of them was what she was wearing. It was a wonderful, comforting smell.

"How far along are you?" she asked softly.

I looked at her up close, glad I was wearing my dark glasses. Crying made me so much uglier. I looked at my hands in my lap and used my fingers to count. "Four days," I finally announced.

It was as though her spine had been skewered from above, she sat upright so fast. "Four *days?*" she echoed. "Don't you mean four *weeks?*"

It had been just four days since I met Squirl on the mountain. Since he beguiled me with his silvery voice, his smile, his body. Just four days. Four weeks ago I hadn't even been born yet.

"Four days," I whispered through my tears. Whether I was now crying at my fate, my sheer love for Squirl or for my unborn child, I had no idea.

She then stood up in front of me, nearly knocking my cup and saucer off the table. "Stand up," she ordered, looking a little like Babe when she was on to something. "Take those glasses off," she continued.

My hands sprang to my glasses and I said, "No, the lights in here—"

"The joke's over, young woman!" She grabbed for my glasses.

She was faster than me and she pulled them off, string and all. With them came my scarf. Immediately I squinted against the light of the chandelier behind her. I sat back down, puffy pink eyes and all.

She also sat down, only on the table and totally unaware that she'd upset my coffee and cake. Her lovely mouth was open, her black eyebrows were arched, and I have to admit, I got a certain amount of satisfaction at seeing her instant horror. It was like getting to say "I *told* you so!" without uttering a single word.

"Here," she said, handing me back my glasses. "You're albino." Apparently the fact that I was also fifty percent Chinese and one hundred percent pregnant by her fifty percent brother eluded her.

I could only nod as I fumbled to put my scarf back on.

"No, don't," she said. "Leave it off. Your hair is beautiful." She took my scarf from me and placed it on the table. Then she walked to the light switch, turned off the lights and opened the window shade so that the soft daylight came in. "There," she said. "I know that's better."

She cleaned the spilled coffee off of the table, then poured me some more, smiling down at me. She said, "Now, let's get back to . . . four days?"

16

Sally rang for Gina and asked for something more substantial to eat. I remembered it was morning and I was hungry. I wondered again if Sally had been up all night. She didn't look like she was tired. She looked beautiful.

Her phone rang and Gina answered it. She started to hand the elegant white phone to Sally, saying it was Mr. Madison. But before Sally took the phone, she did the oddest thing. She walked over to me and asked, "Do you mind?"

Mind? Mind what? I shook my head in a weak no. Then she ran her hand through my hair. She thanked me and went to the telephone, waiting for the man at the other end to say something while she smiled at me and crossed her fingers.

My God, city people are strange, I thought. She finished her conversation and I could tell she'd received some good news.

"Well, my dear, it seems I owe you more than breakfast," she said. "What did you say your name was?"

"Cordelia Hankins. But please, keep it to yourself."

"Oh, I'm going to keep you all to myself," she said. She went on to explain that where she came from, albinos were not only lucky, but cherished as well.

"Where's that? The moon?" I asked.

"New Mexico. In case you couldn't tell, I have a little Indian blood in me. We had legends of albinos in our village and they were always honored. That phone call was from my lawyer. I've been waiting all week for the grand jury to come back. You walk into my life, let me touch your hair and they've dropped the charges."

What albinos had to do with grand juries, I had no idea. In fact, what made a jury grand? But before I could ask, our breakfast arrived and Gina set it up on the table in front of the fireplace.

Sally scooted my chair in for me. Once Sally was seated across the table, once Gina had left, Sally looked at me and asked, "Now, where were we? Oh yes. Now, tell me, dear, how would you know if you're only four days pregnant? What are your symptoms?"

Over breakfast? I watched her eat and I thought Sally was probably the type to discuss anything over breakfast. "Well," I began, "it's been four days since—you know—since we . . ."

"Did it?" she finished for me, her mouth half full of bacon. "Because if it's been just four days since you did it, there's no way in . . . heaven . . . you'd be showing signs by now."

How could she speak so casually? What made her such an expert?

"Have you had babies?" I asked. Let's just see how experienced she is.

She laughed and said no but that this was something she knew a lot about.

"You a midwife or something?" I asked, wondering how a job like that could pay so well.

That also made her laugh. "I've never thought of it that way before, but I guess you could say I've done some midwifing in my day." She looked at me and I thought she could tell, even through my smoked glasses, that I saw nothing funny in my circumstances.

"I'm sorry, Cordelia," she said. "You are absolutely right to be frightened. The world has never looked kindly on a girl in trouble. But, for once, my brother has done the right thing, sending you to me."

Well, he didn't exactly send me, I thought. I just came.

"When can I see him?" I asked.

Sally exhaled, as though thinking about her answer. "How long have you known Squirl?"

"Well, he came to our lumber outfit a couple of months ago, but I've only known him for a few weeks."

"So, he's back on that kick again. Go on."

"And it was just last Sunday we met on the mountain," I further confessed. I knew Catholics confessed things in booths with no windows and I wondered if they also got a secondhand thrill as they recalled their sins, as I was now getting.

"And as a result, you are now pregnant?" she asked, pouring some more coffee for both of us.

"No more for me, thank you," I said. "I've heard too much coffee is bad for babies."

"Trust me, my dear, that coffee isn't going to hurt you or anyone else," Sally said. "Now then, were you a virgin before you met Squirl?"

My God, she got down to the details. I said yes, of course.

"So, it's been four days now and you think you're pregnant? You've already missed a period?"

"Period of what?" I asked.

Sally leaned into me, rested her chin on her hand and then slowly asked, "Has anyone ever told you how these things happen?"

"Um . . . yes," I said, Babe's scowl firmly implanted in my memory, "my stepmother told me. She thinks I'm evil, anyway. I think my father does too. If someone thinks you're evil, you might as well be evil. So I ran away to find Squirl. Is he here? In this house?"

My reunion with her brother seemed to be the last thing Cousin Sally was interested in. She said all in good time, but first perhaps I should see a doctor.

But he was there, in that house. I could *feel* him there. Squirl and me were that way, I just knew it. We could feel each other close by. I stood up and thanked Sally for the breakfast and her kindness. Then I told her that I would see a doctor only after I saw Squirl.

Sally looked at me. I wondered if she was used to having upstart runaways be so stubborn. As far as I saw it, I had lied, run away and risked my life to find Squirl, and I wasn't going to stop now—for Sally, for a doctor or for anyone else.

Sally must have sensed that, heard it in the tone of my voice. I had an odd sort of power over her—almost as though she thought I wouldn't let her touch my hair again for luck if she didn't play her cards just right.

She went to the phone once again, clicked it a few times, then said, "Find my brother and bring him to me. I'm in the sitting room." She came closer and smiled, and I noticed her lip paint had come off. "I'll leave you two alone. But between us two women, will you take some advice? Don't tell him about your—well, about your condition."

I didn't know how else he was going to do right by me, but I agreed, delighted that my love and I were nearly reunited.

Sally left and I put my scarf back on, straightened my glasses and caught a glance of myself sitting, as pretty as I could, in the huge mirror over the fireplace.

It was only a few minutes, but it seemed like forever. The door opened and there he was—my Squirl—dressed in silk pajamas and a robe, half in, half out of the door. He called back to someone down the hall.

"I told you, git on back upstairs, Mimi. I'll be right there soon as I see what the boss wants."

He came in the room and looked around in the dim light. "Why's it so dark in here, Sal?" He punched the light switch on and then he saw me, sitting there on a white and gold brocaded settee, my hands folded demurely in my pregnant lap.

Were my tears tears of joy at seeing him, or tears of terror at what was to become of me, or tears of anger at someone called Mimi? I swiped them away, stood up, smiled a little and said, "It's me—Cordy. I come to see you, Squirl."

Of all the things he could have answered, said, done, he did the worst of all. He just asked, "What for?"

Those two little words—"What for?"—might as well have been two daggers in my heart. He should have known what for. For him. For love.

I knew "what for" really meant "done for."

17

Of all the reactions I'd dreamt Squirl would have when he saw me, this wasn't one of them. This was hardly the time for learning of impending marriage and fatherhood. And what about this Mimi? After all, Squirl was seventeen years old—could it be he was already married? I knew I'd better say something clever and fast.

"How've you been?" I asked. Oh, *that* was clever.

"Hungry," he said, spying my half-finished breakfast and taking a muffin off of my plate. He sat down and looked at me while he chewed, then asked, "Were you done with this?" He held up the remnants of the muffin for my permission before popping it farther into his mouth.

He sloshed it down with coffee, then asked me, "How'd you find this place, anyway?"

"Cousin Sally's in Luna Park in Seattle," I answered. "How hard could it be?" If he'd only known the lengths I'd gone to to get there, though.

"Okay, then *why'd* you find this place?" he asked.

"You have to ask me that?"

He looked a little confused, then said yes, he had to.

"To find *you*, of course," I ventured, still sitting. No rushing into each other's arms, no thank-God-you-found-me kisses. Just chilly, vague questions.

Then he stood up and said, "That father of yours didn't send you, did he?"

"Of course not," I said. "Don't you see, Squirl? I've run away. Cut my tail-holt and run away."

He didn't seem to be listening. He continued, " 'Cause I only owed twenty-two bucks at the company store and if he wasn't bright enough to deduct that from my time and wages, then it ain't like I was walking on a debt. He calculated my pay and I took it. Signed off and everything."

"No one says you stole nothing, Squirl," I said.

"Oh. Good." There was a small silence between us as he folded a napkin. Then he looked at me and said, "You know, Cordy, you might have told me your ol' man was the mill boss. You should have heard the way he talked to me! And it wasn't for riding the flume, neither. Said he'd see to it no mill on the whole West Coast would hire me. Then that Babe, that *thing* he's married to, comes while I'm collectin' my gear and I swear to God, Cordy, if I'd had a gun I would have killed her."

I straightened up, feeling a rage way down deep. If Babe so much as touched . . .

"She slammed me up the side of the bunkhouse so hard it knocked the wind out of me. Now, I know better'n to hit a woman, but hell, Cordy, that stepmother of yours ain't no woman."

"Did you? Did you hit her?"

"Hell no. With what? She had my arms pinned back. Thought she was goin' to kill me. She said she'd rip me limb from limb if I didn't clear out by six o'clock."

None of what he was saying surprised me.

"So ain't no one going to blame you for running away from that father of yours and that monster he's married to," he said, which were the first kind words he'd said so far.

"I wanted out all my life," I said, probably sounding a little martyrish.

"But look, Cordy, this ain't no place for you. I mean, Sally's a jewel and all, but are you sure this is what you want?" He indicated the palace around us.

No, *he* was what I wanted, but not if I had to tell him. I decided to stay on the subject of Sally. "She's your sister, eh?"

"Half sister. She's the successful half of the family, you might say."

"So what's so great about rolling logs in some lumber pond when you can live here? Like a king?" I asked.

He smiled boyishly at me. "Ol' Sister Sal and me get into it every so often. She takes me in, kicks me out. Too bad we don't have the same father, instead of mother. She got all the good sense and money and I got all the talent and looks. Anyhow, I got driftwood in my shoes and I like workin' the logging camps. Like the money, like rollin' logs, and loggers are rotten gamblers. Thought maybe I'd even own my own mill someday."

Squirl had a way of talking, of dreaming, that carried me along with him. I could see it all. Somehow Squirl and me would buy all of Centner's Mill and kick my father and Babe out. But my dream was suddenly broken when the door opened and a little voice peeped, "Squirl? You coming back to bed, honey?"

"Mimi," Squirl said loudly.

"Yes, sugar?" Mimi said back.

"I said I'd be up in a minute."

"But I'm getting sleepy."

"So go to sleep."

Then the door slowly opened further and I saw her, the sleepy Mimi. She was draped in thin layers of almost see-through fabric, with a feathery sort of thing wrapped all around her and golden hair cascading over her shoulders. She looked at me and said, "Hello, sister. You the new seamstress?"

I shook my head and just stared. I followed her gaze back over to Squirl. I think he was just figuring things out as he compared me to her. I wanted to shrink into a little ball of dust and blow away in the gentle draft from the open door.

Then Squirl said to Mimi, "You go back to your room like I told you! This here's a private meeting between me and my friend, who's embarrassed just lookin' at you!"

I was more fascinated by her than embarrassed, actually. But more than anything, I was proud that he was, in a way, defending me by insulting her. Mimi left in a huff, slamming the door. That left us alone once again.

"But you still ain't told me what you're doing here in Seattle," Squirl said, taking a smoke from Sally's table. "Come to see the sights, did you?"

It was now or never: I stood up, walked toward him, took my glasses off and looked directly at him. "Squirl. I come to find you."

His face changed. He put the cigarette out. "You're nothing but a kid. What? Fourteen, you said you were?"

"Age doesn't mean nothing," I said.

"When you're only fourteen it does," Squirl said. "They got laws."

I came this close to telling him about my condition. It was as though Sally had a secret spy hole somewhere in the room, for as soon as I drew breath to inform Squirl of my—of our—condition, she walked in. Had I known more about her place of business, I would have realized a spy hole was exactly what she had.

"Squirl, if you don't want to be late for your appointment, you better get going."

Squirl glanced at a huge grandfather clock in the corner. "She stayin' here?" he asked as he passed by me.

"As my guest," Sally said. "In the corner suite."

"You mean in the sheriff's annex," he said, smiling crookedly. He took a handful of cigars from a silver humidor.

"I mean in the room with the best view, the best bed and a door that locks," Sally answered, taking back the cigars, except the one he'd popped into his mouth.

Squirl grinned around the cigar, backed out, said it was nice seeing me. I wished I could have believed him.

Sally took my hand and asked if I would please consider staying as her guest.

"I have a place over at the West Inn. Paid a week in advance," I said.

"I'll send for your things. I insist you stay here. I promise," she added, "I'll keep you safe."

By noon I was situated in the finest room imaginable. It was just as ornate, just as glorious, as everything else I'd seen since entering Cousin Sally's. It was a room fit for any fairy-tale princess. Maybe I was Cinderella and maybe Sally was my fairy godmother.

The problem with my castle room was that the door she'd mentioned had two locks—one locked from the inside and the other locked from the outside.

18

By noon, my belongings arrived from the West Inn and I quickly changed into my nicest dowdy dress. Shortly after, Gina brought me lunch along with a note on a silver tray from Sally saying a carriage would call for me at two to take me to see a Dr. Ridenour, who was the only physician she would ever trust for matters as delicate as mine.

"Any answer, miss?" she asked. Here she was, probably all of eighteen and calling me "miss" as though I was a grand lady. The closest to miss I'd ever been called was missy and believe me, when Babe or my father called you missy, it wasn't out of respect.

"No. I mean, yes. You can tell Cousin Sally I'll be ready at two o'clock. Where should I meet her?"

"At two this afternoon, miss? Oh, Cousin Sally will be asleep, I'm afraid. Whatever it is you'll be doing, I'm afraid it'll be without Cousin Sally."

I knew Gina could read my face. After all, she had a

brother who was blind and she was probably better at face-reading than most people.

"Don't worry, miss. Cousin Sally likes you and won't let anything happen to you. Otherwise, you wouldn't be here, in this room. This room is for special people only."

Though I tried to rest, I found myself staring at my reflection in one of the gilded full-length mirrors in my room. As I studied myself—my strange colorless eyes and white hair, my odd pale complexion, my smallness—I thought that even with Sally's help there was no way to improve me. Not unless I was going to be one of those miracle girls. You know about those—the ugly ducklings. The kind you overhear adults talking about. "We can't believe little Eva grew into such a lovely thing. She was such an ugly duckling, you know." But ugly little Eva had swan ancestry, not duck, to fall back on. I knew there were no swans in my family. I was going to have to become remarkable in other ways.

Someone knocked on the door. I went to it and that was when I realized it was locked.

"The carriage, miss," I heard Gina say.

"The door must be stuck. It won't open."

"Just a minute, miss." I heard the key go in and watched the ornate crystal knob turn. Gina made no effort to hide the key, which was with others and attached to her waist.

"I'm locked in here?" I asked.

"For your own safety, miss," Gina told me.

"From what?"

Gina was finding my hat and my gloves, which I had laid out on a chair. She gathered them up and handed them to me. "You'll have to ask Cousin Sally, miss. But like I told you, don't be afraid. Cousin Sally's the best friend a girl can have."

"But what if I want to go out?" I asked, wondering why I was growling at the hand that was feeding me.

"Then you ring for someone to open the door," Gina answered simply. "You must hurry now. The carriage is waiting."

"But what if there's a fire or something?" I asked. Up where I came from, fire was the only real, constant fear.

Gina's small smile tried to reassure me. She simply walked to a side window, threw it open, and indicated the heavy metal rigging out there. "Fire escape," she said.

"Oh. Of course," I said.

We took the stairs down. The brass elevator only went to Sally's suite on the third floor.

There I was again—Cinderella. Now riding to the ball in a carriage worthy of a fairy-tale girl. It was black and polished so deeply I saw my reflection as I climbed in. There was a big red emblem and the scrolled letters "C.S." in the middle of the door. The doorman, Simon, helped me in. I thanked him. He now smiled broadly at me and called me miss too. He closed the door and told the driver to take me to Dr. Ridenour.

I prepared myself for a long, comfortable journey and tried to quiet my rising fear. I closed my eyes and listened to the clear, well-shod *clop* of the matched team's feet as they struck the cobbled pavement. I was thinking, if they could only see me now—Babe and my father, the rest of Centner's Mill.

But it wasn't a long journey at all. We went down one block, then stopped. We were in front of the grand admission gates to Luna Park. The driver spoke to the men at the entrance. They tipped their hats, then opened the huge, grilled gates that allowed carriages through. People stepped aside, making way. Two ladies seemed to recognize the carriage and peered inside. I knew a disapproving glance when I saw one. I saw two.

We traveled up the wide brick road, past the huge glassy building I'd seen from the air. The sign called it a natatorium. I had no idea what that was, but I gathered from the life-size cutouts of people in swimming costumes that this was one of those large, indoor heated pools I'd heard about. We continued past a picnic area where a brass band played and people danced. Firecrackers popped, children ran about and lovers walked hand in hand.

Finally we turned away from the gaiety and went down what seemed to be a back alley. Suddenly the fun, the excitement, the smells, just stopped—as though someone threw the master switch. All glitter out front—all shadows out back. Of course, I'd always preferred the shadows. Here again was proof that all bright, gay things have cool, dark undersides. Like all alleys, this was where the people who worked at the park came and went, where deliveries were made, where bets were settled.

What a strange place to have a medical practice, I thought.

We stopped behind a dark, three-story building. Cement stairs led down to a basement doorway.

The driver opened the coach door, helped me out and pointed down the stairs.

"You sure this is the place?" I asked him.

"Bet I brought a hundred girls here," he replied. "I'm to wait around front."

I watched the horses as they gingerly stepped around the corner and back into the sun.

I walked down the steps, thinking I'd gotten into this

mess by myself and I was going to get out of it by myself. I squinted at the writing on the door.

Dr. Ridenour's Medical Cabinet of
Human Oddities, Curiosities and Nondescripts
Medical Advice for the Young Man
Private Entrance

My timid knock was barely audible. So I put some arm into the next try.

Knock. Knock. Knock.

Nothing. Then I lifted my glasses and noticed a small sign on the side wall that said to please ring the bell. I cranked it around, heard the weak *brrrring* and stood back a step. I could hear the nearby rumble of the roller coaster as the cars screamed around a corner.

The door finally opened. An odd little voice said up to me, "Go away. We ain't buying."

The door started to close and I stopped it. The woman might have been small, but she was strong. "Wait a minute," I said. "I . . . I have an appointment."

"I said beat it. This ain't no beauty parlor. . . ."

Again the door started to close.

"No, isn't this Dr. Riden-something's office?" I asked, this time getting my foot in the door.

"Ridenour," she corrected me. The light from behind silhouetted her small, round frame. "What do you mean, you have an appointment?"

"A . . . Sally said for me to come . . ."

What sort of a place was this and what was this creature? Then it hit me—this woman was a dwarf, just like in the

Snow White story. She was dressed in a starched white uniform.

"Sally must be getting desperate, hiring the likes of you,"
she sniffed. She waddled past me, hopped up the steps,
looked up and down the alley, then looked back at me and
said, "Well, what're you looking at? Get on in there before
someone sees you!"

She locked the door, then led the way down a dark hall.
There were no windows and only an occasional light switch.
She'd turn one light on, then turn it off as we would turn
right, then left, down here, over there, passing doors with no
names, no numbers. If this was the doctor's nurse, then what
was he going to be like? And why was I following this gnome
through the maze of short corridors into God knew what?

She finally opened one of the doors. She stood on her
tippy-toes to reach the switch and turned on a weak overhead
light. In the dim room was one chair, one desk, one examination table. No window. It was cold and clammy. I didn't
know if it was the cool air or the strange odors around me
that made me feel a little faint. I went into the room as
instructed. The nurse stood in the doorway, her head just
below the doorknob.

"Sit down," she ordered. "The doctor's in a consultation
right now. Might be a while."

"Could I have a glass of water?" I asked.

"Of course not. And you better not have eaten nothing,
either."

"Not since lunch," I said, my fears rising.

"Oh, that's just great," she grumbled. We looked at each
other with curiosity. She was my first dwarf. Maybe I was her
first albino. Then she asked. "You blind or something?"

"No, just sensitive eyes."

She nodded her head, then said, "Well, have a seat and don't touch nothing."

With that, she walked out, closing the door. I heard her awkward steps down the hall; then I heard another door close. Sally's kind considerations or not, I knew I wasn't going to stay there. I heard the far-off, loud voice of a man and I took my glasses off. Somehow doing that makes me hear better. I'd heard plenty of squeals and squeaks and screams since I'd come to Luna Park. But those were all sounds of fun, delight, excitement. This sounded different.

I slowly opened the door and looked down the hall. The nurse had turned off the lights and it was dark. If she had turned off the lights to prevent my escape, she was dead wrong. The dark didn't scare me one bit. Too bad I hadn't been clever enough to remember the way. All I knew for sure was the voices had come from the left and I had entered from the right.

I was moving slowly down the hall when I heard a door open and close with a slam. I ducked through the first available door. I heard footsteps running down the hallway, followed by another loud door slam.

I leaned against the door, catching my breath. The room smelled horrible, almost vile. But, in case there were still people in the hallway or worse, in case that dwarf had found me missing and was looking for me, I decided to hide deeper in the room. There was a dim light, perhaps coming from a window off in the distance. I longed for fresh air. The stench in the room was a cross between alcohol and Lysol and snake oil. But there were obstacles in my way. They felt like desks or wooden boxes and I worked my way carefully around them toward the distant light.

The light didn't come from a window at all. Well, in a

way it did. But the window was one of those glazed ones in yet another door. What was this place? So many halls, so many rooms. On this door, the word "private" was painted in bold black letters.

I stepped closer, leaned forward and listened. My glasses dangled against my pounding heart. I heard nothing, yet felt a very strange presence, sort of like someone was watching me. Somehow I knew I wasn't alone.

I think I waited on the dark side of that door for at least six lifetimes, working up the courage to either go back or venture forward. Convinced I heard no one on the other side, I slowly turned the knob. Not locked. Was that good or bad?

I pushed gently and edged my nose in and looked around.

Turns out I was right twice: No, there was no one in the room and yes, I was not alone.

19

I had entered a laboratory of some kind. There were long rows of countertops with scientific instruments. They were similar to those I'd seen in our clinic back at Centner's Mill, but there were also rows of jars—some large, some tiny, some arranged neatly in ascending order of size. Each jar was filled with clear fluid.

There were *things* floating in the jars. Formless gray things.

I came closer. Some of the jars were identified with tags pasted on the base. I leaned across the counter for a closer look.

Malformed Human Fetus—Four Months

read the tag. I tried to make out the grayish lump in the jar. All I could clearly define as human was the head. I carefully turned the jar around. A solitary black eye stared out through the fluid, as though gazing placidly past me. I wondered, Can an eye gaze if it's never actually seen?

I carefully approached another jar and looked at the label:

Female Siamese Twins
Born May 11, 1903—Died May 22, 1903

There, tucked together, arm in arm in arm in arm, they hugged each other for eternity in this mausoleum of formaldehyde. To be viewed, to be studied, to be pitied. Yet their faces . . . sweet, peaceful.

What were these things doing here? Then I remembered the writing on the back-alley entrance door—human oddities and nondescripts . . . I supposed that included that dwarf nurse, these jarred-up "things" and maybe even me, another human oddity.

I had to tear my gaze away and get out of this place. I looked around the room for another exit, struggling to hear a sound from somewhere outside. If I concentrated really hard, I could feel the vibration of the roller coaster. I could hear the faraway squeals of summer delight.

There was another door toward the end of the room. I walked through rows of jars of God knows what or God knows who, not daring to look, barely able to keep my eyes straight ahead. Out of here! Cordy, get out!

This door warned "No Admittance," as though that would have kept me from trying. I was in a storage room. I switched on the light, let my eyes adjust to the brightness, then looked around me.

The far shelf had a row of more jars, more lifeless things, chemicals and tools. One large jar was filled with what appeared to be a mass of white cotton. But there was something disturbing and familiar about it. I crept closer and read the label.

**The hair of Unzie,
the Australian Aborigine Albino.
These tresses are over six feet in length
and thought to be
the only sample of Unzie's hair
in the United States.**

Along the side wall there were stacks of old photographs, newspaper articles, handbills and various clippings. It was as though this was a collection all waiting to become a library someday of the malformed, the macabre, nature's little blunders.

There were photographs of fully grown oddities—ones that had avoided the embalmed state—who survived their inadequacies and grew to exhibit themselves, not in a jar, but on a stage. There was Jo Jo the Dog-Faced Boy; Julia Pastrana, the World's Ugliest Woman; followed by an assortment of midgets, legless wonders, rubber-skins and pinheads, and Siamese twins, including Chang and Eng, whom I'd even heard of.

At the bottom of a stack, the yellowed corners of a large handbill peeked out. I gently tugged and pulled it out. It heralded the coming of:

**Dr. Ridenour's Traveling Museum of
Mystic and Medical Anomalies
Education for the Young Man
Cures for Female Complaints**

The poster was illustrated with drawings of bottles of cures, sketches of astonished men, fainting women, happy, healthy children. Then it offered a twice-daily performance by Giganta, the World's Strongest Woman.

Clipped under the poster was an old newspaper photograph and a short article. I pulled it out and read it.

Giganta the Amazon, pictured here with Carlotta the Dancing Dwarf, circa 1905. Giganta was world-famous for her songs and stories and feats of unearthly strength. Sadly, Giganta came to a tragic end. While working in Chicago in 1906, she and her manager-husband argued and in a fit of uncontrollable anger, Giganta bashed in his head, then fled toward Lake Michigan. She was seen crashing into the chilly waters, and in spite of various reported sightings for several years thereafter, she is presumed to have drowned. For many years this case grew in carnival folklore, fueled in part by the curiously large reward of $10,000 for her capture. As of this writing, 1915, it is unknown whether the reward is still valid. All that is really known and remembered about Giganta is her tremendous strength, her terrifying presence and her powerful will.

I walked under the light and closely studied the faded photograph.

Giganta was as huge as Babe.

In fact, Giganta *was* Babe.

I don't know how long I stared at the clipping. I read it again and held it closer to the light, trying to find some reason not to believe what I was rereading. And that photo. Giganta. Murder. Babe. The air grew thick and my heart began to race. I had to get out of there. I stuffed the article deep into the pocketbook tied to my waist, then straightened the photos and articles so that the pile looked undisturbed.

I heard a man call out, "Carlotta! So where is she? This room's empty."

A door slammed. I held my breath. I heard Carlotta, the nurse, call back, "How should I know where that girl went? She probably spooked and ran when she heard that young man go screaming out. I keep telling you to lock them stair doors!"

Then I heard the door open. I whirled around and my elbow must have knocked one of the jars off the shelf. It crashed to the floor and seemed to explode. The contents splattered at my feet.

I don't know what made my head spin—the putrid smell of the chemicals, the horrid things around me or the article about Babe in my pocketbook. The room began to whirl. I don't remember actually hitting the floor, but I recall my last thought as I went down: I had this coming.

20

I awoke in my bed back at Cousin Sally's, thinking my head would explode. As I opened my eyes, I tried to focus and remember where I was. I noticed my hair was all undone, brushed into silvery layers and lying about me. I was wearing silk. I knew silk because once I had a silk scarf my mother had given me. I cherished it. You know silk when your skin touches it. There's nothing like it in the whole world.

The lights were dim and for an instant, I had no idea what time or even what day it was. I don't think I'd ever fainted before, so I wasn't sure if this was how it happened. By the pain in my head and neck, I must have hit something when I fell.

"How are you, my dear?" a man asked. I turned my head and looked at the man sitting next to my bed.

"Who are you?" I asked. "What happened?"

"I am Dr. Ridenour," he replied, taking my wrist and counting my heartbeats against the second hand of his pocket watch. I wanted to pull my hand away, but I had no strength to move.

"What day is it?" I asked.

"Saturday morning. You've had quite a nap."

"I slept for . . . two days?"

"Well, we wanted you to rest and gave you a sedative. Your head is fine. Only a bump," the doctor said.

He put my hand back down on my chest and slowly the hazy recollections came back to me—the place of his practice, those jars of things, those smells.

"Where's Sally?" I asked, not at all sure I wanted to be alone with this Dr. Ridenour.

"I'll get her," he said, walking to the door.

He had a deep voice, thick salt-and-pepper hair and stark blue eyes. He was maybe fifty or so. He opened the door, called for Gina to get Sally and came back in.

"You were quite a worry, young lady," he said, coming back to the bed. I'd only seen two doctors in my life, and both of those were company doctors who wore starched white in their little examination rooms and who seemed ancient and wise and kindly. This man wore a dark suit, obviously expensive, and I thought he looked more like someone who made a fortune using other people's money than a doctor.

I winced when I sat up in bed. My whole body was stiff and uncooperative. "Why?" I asked. "What did I do?"

"Let's wait for Sally, shall we? Would you like a drink of water? Maybe some broth?"

"Am I sick?" I asked, remembering lying in bed just a few days ago, bleeding and wondering about cancer.

"No, you're not sick," he replied, looking down at me.

The other doctors had looked down at me that way, as though because they were medical men and I was a medical mishap, they had a right to their special interest. All I knew for sure was that this Ridenour collected things. How many of those specimens were alive when this doctor first saw them?

I was relieved when Cousin Sally came into the room.

"Well," she said, smiling down at me, "I see our friend is alive and well."

Alive and well, did she say? As opposed to dead and sick? What was going on? And why wasn't Squirl here at my bedside if I'd been so ill?

"What happened, Sally?" I asked as she drew a chair over to the bed. Sally was dressed in possibly the most gorgeous gown I'd ever seen. It was all satins and skirts and swish. She was so beautiful, I was almost embarrassed to be lying there, so white, so—in comparison to her—so odd, so curious, so nondescript.

I looked over and saw Gina standing in the doorway, holding towels and looking at me with concern, I thought. Sally noticed and dismissed her. Maybe I *was* dying after all.

I looked up at the doctor standing at the foot of my bed. "Is it bad?" I asked, my eyes beginning to sting.

Sally smiled, showing lovely white teeth against brilliant red lips. "You knocked over some chemicals that could have been quite dangerous. Thank heavens Dr. Ridenour found you when he did. Plus, that bump on your head didn't help. Anyway, you're going to be just fine," she said. "Isn't that so, Emil?"

Dr. Ridenour nodded. "Just fine, my dear."

"And the baby?" I asked, finally thinking about someone else besides me.

They looked at each other, then Sally said, "Cordelia, there is no baby."

I turned my head away. I'd known I would lose it. Or maybe it was in a jar now, in that place of horrors. I looked up at the doctor. Sally took my hand to return my eyes to her. "Cordelia, there never *was* a baby."

"But," I whispered to her, "Squirl and me—we did *things.*"

"Well, whatever *things* you did, losing your virginity wasn't one of them," she stated.

"But Babe said if I . . . and I did . . . all I . . ." I looked up to the doctor, then leaned closer to Sally and whispered to her, "and I *bled.*"

"And who's this Babe? Some little playmate? Some imaginary friend, perhaps?" Sally asked, folding her arms across her chest.

I burst out laughing. Babe—some little playmate! I put my hand to my mouth to quiet myself and answered, "Babe is my stepmother."

The mention of her name brought back a vision of Giganta—that article and the poster. My smile faded.

Sally asked, "Your stepmother told you all that nonsense? She ought to be horsewhipped for lying to you like that!"

Yes, I silently agreed. For that and about a million other lies.

"Too bad there's no gutter where you came from. At least there you'd have learned proper about the birds and the bees." Then she added, "I have a book I want you to read after Dr. Ridenour leaves."

Which he did after jotting down some notes on a clipboard. Once we were alone, Sally said, "I'm going to ring for tea."

But I didn't want tea. I wanted to be alone so I could find

my pocketbook and read again about Babe's past. "I think I'd rather just take a bath. Is that okay?"

"Certainly, my dear. I'll have Gina—"

"No, I can manage. Really. Thanks anyway."

Sally opened a drawer, pulled out a book and handed it to me. She left, saying she'd be happy to answer any of my questions tomorrow.

But Sally couldn't answer the questions I had. I found my pocketbook, still dangling from my skirt belt. I pulled out the article, reread it, then—hearing Gina at my door—stashed the article deep in my top dresser drawer.

So there I was, in a room fit for royalty. Betrayed by Babe for keeping me so stupid. Betrayed by my father for keeping Babe.

But not pregnant.

Which changed everything.

21

You know what kind of a book it was that Sally had given me? It had *color* plates of human anatomy, both male and female. I hate to say this is how I got my education regarding sex: reading a textbook in a stranger's bathtub. But if it wasn't for Sally and that book, no telling how long I would have gone on thinking brazen little flume-flyers who roll around in the mud and open their mouths to a kiss get blood and babies for their passionate trouble. I could have slipped down under the water and drowned myself from embarrassment as I realized how simple things in nature were and how ignorant those back at Centner's Mill had kept me.

The truth was: no baby. And the truth, so the saying goes, will set you free.

I wasn't thrilled to learn, though, that my bleeding would become a monthly situation. The book gave a list of popular references to it and, now that I knew the truth, I could look back and understand the conversations of women I'd overheard.

"I'm expecting a visit from my little friend."

"I got the curse of Eve."

"The monthlies are killing me."

"It's that time of the month."

And I'd thought they were talking about paying bills.

But mostly, not being with child changed me and Squirl. Of course, since I hadn't told him yet, I had nothing to take back, nothing to explain. Nor did I have anything to hold him by.

After everything I'd been through in the last few days, the worst of it was knowing I was going to lose Squirl. No doubt he'd learned of my accident at the doctor's. The chemicals, hitting my head. He hadn't come dashing to my side.

So, a few hours later, when there was a gentle knock on my bedroom door and I heard Squirl's voice calling me, I first leaped to my feet. Even though I was bathed and dressed, I got back into bed. I didn't want him to know how eagerly I'd been anticipating any small favor he might bestow on me. No more acting like an idiot, Cordy. Be distant, cool, be smart now.

"Come in," I said, patting the covers down around me.

Squirl poked his head into the room and looked around.

I fastened the top button of my blouse and arranged my long hair around my shoulders. He'd never really seen my white hair in all its long, combed-out glory. I wondered if he'd think it was old-looking and ugly. Why couldn't it be golden, like Mimi's, or that wonderful deep auburn like Sally's?

"Sally says you're under the weather," Squirl said.

"I'm all right," I answered.

He stood looking at me until the silence made me uncomfortable. "What are you looking at?" I finally asked.

Squirl snapped out of his stare and answered, "You. Your hair. You know, Cordy, that hair really is . . . really is . . ."

"White," I finished for him. It was white. That's all it was.

"Yes, but . . . I don't know, maybe it's the light in here."

He walked from the foot of the bed and pulled up a chair next to me. "So, what are your plans?" he asked.

Well, I had none, but I said, "Work, I guess."

"Here?"

"I don't know. I suppose I could do book work for Sally, if she needs me."

Squirl crossed his legs and ran his hand along the edge of my nightstand. "Do you have any idea what kind of place this is?"

I smiled, looking around the room. "It's a palace. A fairyland."

"No, I mean, do you know what kind of *business* Sally's in?"

"Restaurant and lodging?" I asked back. Deep down inside, I must have known otherwise.

"Besides that," Squirl went on, leaning toward me.

I looked away and asked, "Is Mimi a whore?"

"Yep, Mimi's a whore. From what Sally was sayin' I wasn't sure you even knew what a whore was."

"A whore's a girl who sells herself, either for money or for barterable goods, for sexual pleasure," I stated, picking up Sally's book and reading, " 'Chapter Nine—Sexual Deviances and Moral Considerations.' "

He took the book from me and noticed it was wet.

"I dropped it in the bathtub," I explained.

"Why? Too hot to handle?" he asked, leafing through it, stopping to gaze at probably the same color plate that had made me drop the book in the tub. He put the book down, then gave me that grin—the one I fell in love with on the mountain that wonderful Sunday. He said, "I know other ways to earn a livin'. Legal ways that don't have nothin' to do with Chapter Nine or Sally or Mimi or nothin'."

"I can type," I said, thinking that made me quite a commodity. "Maybe I could work for a lawyer or something."

"You ain't gonna type nothin' for no lawyer, if I have anything to do with it," Squirl said, slipping into his casual backwoods speech.

"Do you?"

"Do I what?"

"Have anything to do with it?"

He paused, looked at me, reached over and picked up a lock of my hair. "I got some ideas how you and me might do all right for ourselves."

"How? Doing what?" I asked, pulling my lock of hair back. This was far too important a conversation to have the distraction of my hair between us.

"Can you sing?" he asked.

"No. Why?"

"Well, how about can you dance?" he asked.

"Why? What for?"

"Well, I got to thinkin' . . . you could do all right if you put yourself on display."

All I could see was a row of huge jars and me floating in one of them.

My face must have shown that, because Squirl immediately jumped in with, "I mean, a girl as unusual—as unique—as you. No tellin' how far you could go. And all's you'd have to do is stand onstage, billow your hair out some and maybe, you know, sing a song or dance a dance. Maybe recite some poems."

I looked at him and ran through my mind the photos of those human oddities I'd seen advertised in the old traveling posters in the laboratory. I remembered the sample of the Australian man's—Unzie's—hair. "Oh, you mean sell myself either for money or for barterable goods."

"Yes!" Squirl said, slapping his knee. "I was just talkin' to Dr. Ridenour and he says you're very rare, bein' both half Chinese and all albino. We could work up something that you were a Chinese princess, say, sold into slavery and cursed with ancient secrets—"

"No," I said, cutting him off.

"Why not?" he asked. Did he really think I would agree to being . . . what? An exhibit?

"Because I can't sing and I can't dance and I don't tell stories and I'm not a very good liar." I thought that covered things pretty well.

"Look, Cordy, Ridenour's puttin' together a new Ten in One."

"What's that?"

"Well, it's sort of a sideshow, like you see at the circus or at a carnival." I gave him a blank look. "Never even been to a circus, have you? Well," he said, standing up. "No wonder you're all spooked. Okay, you and me have a date tonight. I'm takin' you to Luna Park. How can you make a decision as big as this without knowing what it's all about?"

He left, saying he'd pick me up that afternoon at four P.M. sharp and I should be prepared for the "funnest night of my life."

Alone in my room, I tried to put things in the order of their importance. How can life drag on so for fourteen awful, long, dull years and then, *BAM!* within the time of one short week, everything move so fast, be so scary and yet so exciting?

22

Sally wasn't thrilled I was going out that afternoon. She was worried it was too soon, and what about that lump on the back of my head? I told her, since we'd be at Luna Park, if I started to feel bad we'd either come straight back or we'd slip into Dr. Ridenour's. Maybe I was a better liar than I thought.

Sally sent Gina in with some clothes she thought would fit and I knew I'd have to start repaying Sally for all her kindnesses. I went to the huge closet, found my satchel and counted my money. I wondered how much lodging in a place of this magnificence might cost. I was right about one thing: I was going to have to find a job soon.

I thought about Squirl's eager suggestion that I put myself on display to be a curio in Dr. Ridenour's collection. "Curio"—curious word. Hardly a word to use on Babe or Giganta or whoever she was.

I locked my door and went to my dresser. Sitting by my window in the strong summer light, I dissected the article line by line. I pulled out my magnifying glass, which made reading the fine, faded print easier. Carlotta the Dancing Dwarf—Ridenour's nurse.

Remember what I said about not being able to tell how old a woman like Babe is? Well, she looked nearly the same in the photograph. Maybe that's the barter . . . sure, you're a freak, but you're an ageless freak. I guess that's a concern for beauties like Mimi and Sally . . . everyone notices when your beauty fades.

I read the article for the eleventeenth time. No one could doubt she *could* kill a man with her bare hands. Babe was Hercules, Samson and Attila the Hun. And who knew more than me what her fits of temper were like? Sure Babe could kill.

The words that really caught my attention, though, were "reward for her capture." I imagined leading a posse into Centner's Mill, going into the house, collecting Babe using a huge net and hauling her back to the big-city sheriff like Teddy Roosevelt might have dragged home a bagged elephant. I saw her on trial and me as a witness to her evil character. I saw my father standing on the sidelines—helpless for the first time in his life. And the outcome all in my hands.

I saw myself collecting thousands of dollars off the head of Babe. I would be rich on blood money. I'd fan myself with thousand-dollar bills as I walked past my father, saying, "See you around, ol' Red, ol' pal, ol' buddy. If you're ever in the Puget Sound, do drop in."

There was a knock on my door. Four o'clock. It was Squirl. I snapped out of my fantasy of revenge and rewards. I stuffed the article into my dresser drawer, way in back, knowing it would take me several long nights to figure out what to do about Babe.

For now, it was our secret—Babe's, Giganta's and mine.

"You ready?" Squirl asked as I opened the door. "No, you ain't ready."

"Yes, I am," I said, stuffing my braided hair into my cap, watching him walk past me. He went to the arrangement of carnations on my sitting room table and plucked the largest, whitest one. Then he came over to me and placed the flower in the lapel of my jacket. "There. Now you're ready." He opened the door and asked, "Shall we?"

Had he commanded the flower to jump out of the vase, fly to me and place itself in my lapel, I wouldn't have been surprised, such was Squirl's charm. I smiled at him and walked out the door.

Squirl said that since it was Saturday night, the carriage was not available. "You don't mind walkin', do you?" he asked with a sly grin. "I seem to recall you could hike up a whole mountain and not think a thing of it."

The late afternoon was warm and the breeze off Puget Sound was lovely. Even though it was several hours before dusk, the lights of Luna Park were already on and shining, as though beckoning, teasing those still in the hot city: "I'm here, I'm waiting for you, see? I'm all aglow."

The smells were beckoning too. There were several vendors' carts and wagons lining the streets around Luna Park, each offering a tempting delight. Yes, I'd had popcorn, but never smothered in caramel. Yes, I'd had apples, but never encrusted with red cinnamon candy. Yes, I'd had clams, but never fried and dipped in English malt vinegar. By six, I thought I would explode, and we hadn't even entered the gates of Luna Park itself.

Squirl said we should see the waterfront sights first, in the daylight. Stroll the lanes, sample the food outside first. Then enter the park as dusk fell around us. Luna Park, he said, was magical in the dark.

He was right. Just as the sun was setting above the Olympic Mountains, just as the sky glowed in the pinkness promising a warm evening, just as the breeze off the Sound calmed, we paid and entered the park. The noises were louder, more exciting, as though in order to compensate for the darkness the sounds had to increase.

The entire place was Christmas, New Year's Eve and the Fourth of July, all rolled into one and glowing with lights. Everything was lit! The entrances of the various buildings, the trees, the sidewalks. One hardly knew where to begin.

Squirl had it all planned out, though. He spared no expense and I let him do it. I watched the dollars roll, knowing those were the same dollar bills that I had counted, recorded, placed in the cash box, stored in the safe, in my father's office back at Centner's Mill. I was getting something of a thrill watching them being spent so lavishly—on me, no less—and on pure amusement, perhaps even forbidden amusement, according to the banner we were now passing under.

It read:

Welcome to Dr. Ridenour's
Carnival of Mystic Delights
No Unescorted Ladies
No Children

23

It was almost as though you could feel the air around you change when you walked under that banner. I could swear the sounds outside muted, then melted, then merged into the sounds ahead of us. The smells seemed to change too. No longer the aromas of sweet distraction, but now the come-hither smell of strong coffee and foreign spice. As though the banner over our heads wasn't sufficient warning, there was a uniformed guard on either side of the turnstile, scaring off curious youths, turning back ladies without a gentleman's arm. I watched two ladies, giddy and curious and maybe even drunk, run off and in the blink of an eye return on the arms of two soldiers.

Of course, I'd already journeyed through Dr. Ridenour's chamber of horrors, so little could make my knees weaken, I thought. After all I had been through in the last week, nothing was going to frighten me.

Squirl found us some coffee. He said it was Turkish and it

was so strong I wondered if even the men back at Centner's Mill could have drunk it without their eyeballs popping out, like mine seemed to be. We sat at a table built around the trunk of a tree and watched the activity around us. The strings of lights danced lightly on a breeze off the water, and it was really a lovely night. Squirl said we should walk to the right and circle around and that would leave the best for last.

"What's the best?" I asked.

"I don't know. I can never decide between the body of John Wilkes Booth and the Dance of the Seven Veils," Squirl said, looking rather concerned.

We returned our cups to the coffee wagon and continued on our way. Squirl was nothing but charming and I was proud to take his arm. Other girls—well, I guess you could call them women—looked at him, then at me. I know they thought he was simply entertaining his poor blind cousin and they smiled kindly at him, almost as if to say "Take her home, then take me anywhere." They didn't know I could see them almost as plainly as they could see me. At times like this, I loved my smoked glasses.

But Squirl didn't seem to pay any attention to them. He was so handsome, I'm sure he was used to their bold stares. Anyway, I was proud to be his that evening.

And, I am proud to say, I didn't squirm or scream at any of the sights I saw. Although, God knows, I was probably just as amazed as anyone there. The first thing we saw was Nah Nuk the Seal Face Boy. His face was all brown and misshapen, half human and half—well, he did look something like a seal, and he just sat there in the middle of the stage and yelped at his "trainer"—a man in a tuxedo and a top hat. What was really odd was Nah Nuk swallowed fish whole, just like a seal would. No kidding. I think that was the worst part. The audience groaned and gasped when he did that. A six-inch fish. Gone in one swallow.

Squirl whispered in my ear, "Don't worry. He throws 'em up after the show. They're still whole and everything. He uses 'em again for the next show. Nuk's got great regurgitation. A lot of his face is just makeup and putty, but he does have one heck of a birthmark to start with."

I felt the coffee and cotton candy in my stomach shaking hands. Some ladies brought hankies to their mouths. But I held my own.

The next tent was easier on the stomach. The pitchman outside said the fire-eater inside his tent had entertained the kings and queens of Europe and was the "*Toast* of three continents. Get it, ladies? Toast? Ha-ha-ha!"

When Squirl came up to pay our admission, ten cents apiece, the man looked down from his stage and said out of the side of his mouth, "I heard the great Squirl was back. Go on in, kid. Take the lady, too. My treat."

The act started and I was quickly mesmerized by the fire-eater in front of us. He really ate fire. He took long gulps of flaming swords. He'd blow flames out of his mouth, too. Once, he even asked us to move aside—said we were too close and it was too dangerous when he took a swig of gasoline and then lit it while he blew flames out over the audience. He was pretty funny about it too. He asked if anyone wanted a cigarette lit or needed a wart burned off—no extra charge.

From there Squirl took me to Jim-Jam the Human Pincushion. This fellow poked pins in himself. He sure lived up to his billing, because he looked like a regular pincushion by the time the act was finished. And not one drop of blood anywhere.

Then we saw a set of Siamese twins—Valerie and Vonetta—stuck together at their hips. They sang songs and did a little act where one wanted to go this way and one wanted to go that way.

Squirl again whispered in my ear. "But no one's ever seen 'em naked, so none of us is sure they really *are* connected."

"Isn't that dishonest?" I asked back.

"Well, they *are* close twins, so Doc Ridenour don't give a hoot. Can't believe everything you see in a place like this."

I remembered those words. They helped when we were viewing the body of John Wilkes Booth and listening to the pitchman's grind about him while he walked around the fancy casket. He said it was common knowledge at the state department that Booth didn't burn up in a barn fire like the history books said. That he was helped out of Washington and taken someplace else with a new identity and given a new life. Course, he had to give up acting. He died in aught-two and would be glad to know he was once again onstage, although his deep, rich acting voice was missed. The spiel went something like that. Then we were told we could walk around the coffin and inspect the body. The man said that anyone who fainted easy shouldn't come any closer, because he'd run out of smelling salts the last show.

I went up. I'd seen plenty of corpses, including the pickled ones in Ridenour's basement. All I can say is it was a man, he was dressed as though he'd stepped right off the stage in 1865 and he was most definitely dead. His skin was yellow and leathery and I imagined he could have been just about anyone *but* John Wilkes Booth. Squirl must have read my skeptical face. He pulled me away from the coffin and whispered, "Ain't Wilkes at all. It's an unclaimed body Dr. Ridenour ordered for medical study, only *he* don't study it. Everyone else does."

Somehow that made perfect sense.

The last act was Salome and her Dance of Seven Veils. And there *were* seven of them. I counted them as she stripped them off and wrapped them around Squirl's neck. The men in the audience were hollering. I'd heard about acts such as these in burlesque. The fact that it was billed as a famous historical reenactment didn't do much to fool anyone. Lots of ladies refused to even enter. There were some benches out front for them to sit and wait for their escorts. I wouldn't have missed it for the world, since my biblical training was so neglected.

She didn't really take her clothes off. If you caught Salome in the right light, you could tell she had on some sort of skintight body thing, complete with painted-on navel and even nipples, which looked a little off center, I thought as I recalled PLATE IX in Sally's book. Perhaps she had to visit the bathroom before the show and didn't get everything back on just right. Anyway, she was nearly offstage by the time she took off veil number seven.

Squirl told me he thought Salome had put on weight since her last baby. I forgave her her lopsided chest.

I don't know when I'd ever had so much fun. I loved it all. It was exciting and mysterious and hilarious all at the same time. I rather liked being among human oddities and I didn't feel nearly so different, watching these people on display. So when Squirl suggested we stop by Countess Polanski's tent to get our fortunes told, I was all for it.

"Come in," a voice commanded after Squirl pulled a bell requesting an audience. Squirl opened the tent flap for me and the inside was glowing in candlelight. There were candles everywhere. My first thought was, Do I really want to sit in this firetrap? But I thought, If this Countess Polanski can see the future, then no doubt she'd be the first to know if the tent was going to burn down.

She was busy looking at the odd cards in front of her. "Welcome, wayfarers, to Countess Polanski's humble tent. Cards, palms or tea leaves?" she asked, without looking up. She spoke with a thick accent and her words sounded like she'd said them six million times.

"It's me, Halbie, you can drop the act," Squirl said.

The fortune-teller looked up, saw Squirl, then stood up and shook his hand.

"Squirl, my old friend, where've you been?" the countess asked, strange accent suddenly gone, and the voice now lower. I stared as closely as good manners would permit. I watched them shake hands and noticed the countess had huge hands and she seemed stoutly built.

The countess was a man, dressed as a Gypsy woman. Imagine my face. Never in a million years would it have occurred to me that a man would dress up as a woman. I'd seen many women, even Sally, don men's clothes for all sorts of reasons—work, comfort, nothing else clean—but never, never had I seen anything like this. Cousin Sally's book hadn't covered this one.

I was introduced to Halburton Polanski—once known worldwide as Polanski the Great, the Great Halburton and now Countess Polanski, but I could call him Halbie. I was asked to sit down. Squirl was offered a stimulant—brandy, I think. Polanski joined him and gave me a cup of tea.

"I heard you were back. Nobody thought those woods

could keep you for long. Meet any . . . lumberjacks?" he asked with a lusty smile.

"Halbie, a million times I told you: I don't go that direction." Squirl looked at me, touched my hand and said, "I like women."

Halbie's painted mouth frowned and he said, "Well, I do too, but—"

"But nothin'," Squirl broke in. "Look, if I ever change my mind, you'll be the first one I ask, okay? Now, how's about a little fortune-telling?"

"Well, let her finish her tea," Halbie Polanski said. "You take your time, sweetie. Let the leaves just settle." He turned up the oil lamp on the table and took a closer look at me. "My, you're an odd little thing, aren't you? Where'd you find her, Squirl?"

"Among the . . . lumberjacks. Take your glasses off, Cordy."

After what I'd seen that night, why not? I did and let the fortune-teller look at me straight-on.

"Oh, look how her eyes dance! Marvelous! And her hair?" he asked, leaning forward to take my cap.

"White as snow," Squirl said proudly.

The fortune-teller settled back and just looked at me, smiling, astonished and, I think, quite impressed. "Oh, we can't let this one slip by us."

"Well, Cordy's pretty new to all this," Squirl said. He drank the last of my tea for me and handed the cup to Countess Halbie. "Here, what does it say? Look real close."

The fortune-teller put his glasses on and examined the tea leaves. "Hmmmmm," he said. "This is strange."

"What?" I asked.

"I see both fame and fortune. Usually I'll see one or the other, but very seldom both." He put the cup down and added, "I better double-check." He took a deck of cards and placed them in an assortment in front of him. "Um-hum," he said, as though consulting with another doctor for a final diagnosis. "I was right. There's fame *and* there's fortune." He pointed the cards out to me as though I would need to see this for myself.

I looked at Squirl and he winked and grinned back at me.

"I knew it," Squirl said, now leaning into me and studying my face. "I knew it from the first day I saw you!"

I hadn't ever been on the receiving end of the look he was now giving me—admiring, proud and as though I was his most precious possession.

I adored it.

24

Within a week the predictions Halbie had made from reading tea leaves and playing with cards began to come true. I was in my room at Sally's, counting my remaining money and my options. With the blessed news of no blessed event, I could see clearer and farther now. Who could dream of going back to the mountains after tasting life in the city? A life such as this? Seattle's excitement or Centner's Mill's sameness? Cousin Sally's approval or Babe's scorn? My father's suspicious glances or Squirl's seductive smiles?

This was my chance—whatever had brought me to Seattle didn't matter now. What mattered was I was here! I was someplace magical where people saw me in a different light. I recalled the flash of Squirl's smile when Halbie said, "Fame and fortune." Are there two more perfect words together? But the words can be spelled out in big block letters at the bottom of my teacup and still not give a hint as to how I was going to get there. Fame and fortune doesn't just *happen*.

I had to *do* something, *become* someone, although I got the feeling Sally would have been delighted to have me stay right there, in that sumptuous room, where she could breeze in, run her hands through my hair and then count her stars, all lucky because of me.

It was all beyond me. My hair had never brought me any luck at all. If anything, it had brought me only teasing and the bad luck that comes when you know you're, well, a genetic error. But maybe that was changing, with the help of Countess Halburton Polanski.

There was a knock on my door. I doubted it was Sally, because she'd been in earlier to pay a visit and to ask if I'd like to join her for dinner that evening. A small, intimate affair with some close friends, she said, but I'd need something new and white and wonderful to wear. Naturally, I agreed, even after I learned that Squirl was not one of the guests.

But it was Squirl at my door. He'd brought Halbie, whom over the week I'd gotten to know. I sincerely liked him. In a way, I think I understood him more than most. And I trusted him, even though he made his meager living fooling people.

Squirl must have come into some money, for he had taken to wearing summer tans and whites. You would have had to be blind not to notice his dashing good looks. No, I'll bet even blind people could *feel* the glow of Squirl's presence. Halbie, on the other hand, was wearing a lovely silk brocade dress, a little tattered and probably too dressy for the middle of the afternoon. But in Luna Park, who cared? Who noticed? If you could overlook the fact that Countess Polanski was a man, all sorts of dragging hems and other fashion errors could go unnoticed.

I asked them to join me in my sitting room.

"I got a proposition for you," Squirl stated, upfront and matter-of-fact. "Cordy, we think you have what it takes."

"For what?" I asked.

"Ridenour paid me a little visit," he went on.

"Oh, let me tell her," Halbie said. His eyes were brimming with a lovely mischief. "All of us think that, with the right training, with the right costuming and staging, you could be the next Katerina McMaster Bishop."

I looked at Squirl over my glasses, which were beginning to slip down my nose.

"Who?"

"Katerina McMaster Bishop. Only one of the greatest mind readers and seers of Europe. Why, until her untimely death, she was the next Nostradamus."

"How come she couldn't *see* her untimely death, if she was so great?" I asked.

Squirl and Halbie looked at each other. Obviously, I didn't get it.

"She didn't see her death because it was an *act*. It's all an act, Cordy," Squirl explained. "But with me as your manager, Halbie as your teacher and Ridenour to promote you, there's no tellin'—"

"Wait a minute. Just what are you suggesting? That I get on the stage and do what? Tell fortunes?"

"No, no, my dear," Halbie said. "Much more than that. *I* tell fortunes. Any goop can do that. You. You can *make* fortunes. *Bring* fortunes."

I looked skeptically at them.

"We want you to call upon the mystical power of your hair and your eyes," Squirl said. "We can't miss. It's all over Luna Park about the luck you've brought Sally, just livin' under the same roof! Don't you see? It's a natural. Don't you know the gift you've been given?" Squirl asked, touching my hand. "Don't you know the money we could make? The countries we could visit? The heads of state we could dazzle?"

"I told you the other day, Squirl. I am not going to exhibit myself."

"This ain't exhibiting, Cordy," Squirl said.

"It's not? Then what is it?"

Halbie and Squirl looked at each other again.

"Well, it's a service. Sort of. You'd be doin' folks a service," Squirl said.

"And it's more than that. It's sheer, wonderful entertainment, Cordy," Halbie added. "Honey, when people come to me to have their fortunes read, I send them away with hope and joy for their futures. I never tell them the *truth*. The truth they get every living, working hour. I only tell them something good, positive, uplifting." He then leaned into me and added, "I entertain them."

"Yeah. See?" Squirl said.

"And it's all so easy," Halbie continued. "Why, in two weeks I could teach you every trick of the trade."

"But I'm only fourteen. Who would ever listen to me? No one listens to kids, no matter what kind of hair they have. No matter how entertaining they are." I was already forgetting how easily I'd duped folks into believing I was a war widow.

"All the better," Squirl answered. He stood up and, as though making an announcement to the world, said, "Introducing Cordelia—Daughter of the Orient, Mystic Child of the Ancients—who, by the power of her innocence and colorless eyes and the strength of her white hair, sees all, knows all."

Halbie joined in and they both said dramatically, "Tells all."

Then Halbie said softly, "You could do it. You really could, honey."

Squirl came to my side, kneeled and looked closely at me. "We could make a fortune."

"You'd be famous."

There they were again—those two words: fortune and fame. What a sweet, familiar note they struck, for hadn't I been, just an hour earlier, rolling those two words around my imagination?

"Is that why you took me to have my fortune told that night?" I asked Squirl. "You two have been planning this all along, haven't you?"

Halbie said, "In show business, you have to make your own opportunities. I'll never make it big, sweetie," he said, touching his false-front chest sincerely. "But I can help *you* make it big."

"I don't know . . ." I wavered. "I think I have . . . to think it over."

"Take all the time you need and ask me anything," Squirl said. "It'll be easy. Like fallin' off a log. God knows we both know how to do that!"

"It'll be fun," Halbie added, touching my hand lightly.

They left after we agreed I would meet them at Dr. Ridenour's the next afternoon with my answer.

You know that expression? I don't know who said it: Some people are born great and some become great and others have greatness thrust upon them.

After the events of that evening, at Sally's intimate dinner, I was soon to become great the third way.

25

The dress Sally had sent up to my room was the most elegant of creations. The fact that people spent so much money on frills still astounded me. The skirt was high, almost midcalf. At first I thought I'd actually grown a little. Then I remembered Paris hemlines were higher that summer and, yes, I was wearing something that had been created in France. I cringed at the idea of wearing so much white, thinking it would only make me look even more like a ghost. But the deep blue collar and satin trim were stunning and I carefully slipped into the dress.

Sally had sent over some hair combs, but I had no idea how to use them. My hair was thick and coarse and difficult to deal with. I could have built a bridge with all the pins it normally took to pile my hair up high. That was why I always wore my cap—it was so much easier to just stuff it all in. I tried six ways to Sunday to build it into something, finally throwing a handful of pins across the room in exasperation. So I just braided it in and out of a blue ribbon down the back and put the combs in along the side.

I looked at myself in the mirror. Turned around. My eyes glanced at the face paint Sally had also sent over for me to experiment with. Dare I? I looked at the palette of gentle colors. One little sweep of pale blue around my eyes and suddenly my eyes looked gray, not pink. Then I dusted my cheeks with a rose powder. Too much at first, so I washed it off and started again. Just a little this time. A far cry from the brownish stains the coffee grounds gave me. Next I painted my lips, being careful to stay within the contours. Hmmm. I hadn't realized my lips were so full.

I put on my smoked glasses, switched on the overhead lights and went to the full-length mirror to get the whole picture of my dress, my hair, my face. I started at my feet and slowly, bravely looked up. Who was that staring back at me? I lowered my glasses to make sure I saw what I was seeing.

"Look, Gert," I said to my doll on the mantel, unable to take my eyes off my reflection. "Look. I'm pretty." The word "pretty" was just a faint whisper, as though I didn't dare say it out loud. But I *was* pretty. Delicate and almost porcelain. And one of a kind.

Sally met me in the corridor and stopped to look at me.

"Cordelia," she said, taking my hands and stepping back. "Lovely. Just lovely."

But she reached for my glasses, asking, "Do you really need these, dear?"

I hesitated, then let her take them, fold them and slip them into my pearl-beaded purse. "No," I said. "I guess I don't."

She looked closely at what I had done to my face, how I

had placed the hair combs and ribbon in my hair. She gently smudged my eyelids, saying, "Here, let's just blend this in a little more . . . Perfect."

"I don't look . . ." I stopped and thought I should be careful. I didn't want to insult Sally by suggesting I looked like a whore.

She read my mind. "No, you look just the way a girl like you should look. I wouldn't let it be any other way." She took my arm. "Come. The gentlemen are waiting."

The dinner Sally was having was quite formal. Not like the casual affairs she'd hold in her set of rooms. This was in a large room with fireplaces on either end and two beautiful chandeliers hanging down from a ceiling that was covered with paintings. By the mirrors along the wall, I thought this must have been a ballroom. The room could have seated probably a hundred people, but in the center of all this lavishness was a small but elegant table set for six. Four men rose as we walked in. Two helped me with my chair, me at one end of the table and Sally at the other.

I felt like the Queen of Sheba. The men remained standing while Sally introduced them to me. Dr. Emil Ridenour, of course, I had already met. I wasn't at all sure I wanted him there, but he was. He looked even more devilish in his tuxedo. Then I met the three other gentlemen. One was a newspaper publisher. The man next to him was some sort of politician, a lieutenant something. Maybe governor. Sally said no matter what else he was, he was first and foremost her lawyer, Sander Madison. The last gentleman was Duncan A. Daniels, chief of the Seattle police, politically also known as good ol' DAD.

It didn't take Sally very long to get down to case cards.

"I'm sure you gentlemen have noticed Cordelia's rather unique appearance," she said, taking a sip from a wineglass.

"Yes, very lovely," one man said.

"And quite rare," Dr. Ridenour added, touching my hand. I hoped he wasn't going to tell them how this unique, quite rare dinner guest had, just up until a few days ago, thought a girl became pregnant by riding a log down a flume and rolling around in the mud.

"Cordelia has many gifts," Sally continued.

From there, the conversation turned from me and my supposed gifts to the politics of Seattle and the State of Washington. To be honest, I was bored and just trying to keep up with the various kinds of food that were served. I did everything Sally did. While they were talking of elections and recounts and scandals and newspapers, I was making sure I was using the right fork or spoon.

Sally did her best to include me in the conversation, but she must have known it was all over my head. Why had she invited me there in the first place?

Finally, over the last luscious course—chocolate mousse— Sally said, "Since Cordelia is new to the area, I'm sure she hasn't had the chance to fully realize your current political predicament, Duncan."

Uh-oh, I thought. I hadn't been paying much attention to the political part of the conversation. Don't tell me they want *my* opinion on politics! All in all, as elegant as that night had been, as regal as I felt in those clothes, I really would rather have been riding the roller coaster with Squirl or listening to Halbie's stories of his strange and colorful past.

Then Chief of Police Daniels turned to me and smiled a

bit uneasily. "I'm afraid I don't take these little eccentricities of Sally's as seriously as she does. You know, like that voodoo her man Simon got her into."

"Oh, don't forget the time she was holding séances," the newspaperman added. "Remember when she brought in that famous medium and charged five hundred bucks a seat just to talk to our dearly departed?"

"Hey, she got Abe Lincoln on the line for *me*," Daniels said, laughing.

Then the newspaperman continued, "But Sally, my dear, as long as you pay for your full-page ads on time, for which I am eternally grateful, I shall support any new craze you find."

"Laugh if you must, gentlemen," Sally said with a cool smile.

What were they talking about? I looked at Sally, bewildered. She explained, "Cordelia, dear. Our poor friend Dunckie is really up against the wall this time. If that vote for recall comes through, then I'm afraid we'll all come to grief. It certainly can't hurt if you let him have a *small* touch."

I put down my fork. "Touch of what?" I asked, looking at my empty plate. All four men broke out in laughter.

I could feel my face redden.

"Sally," Chief Daniels said, lifting his glass, "of all the amusements you've provided me over the years . . . are you suggesting this charming young thing can—what?—bring enough luck to turn the tide of an election?"

Sally wasn't laughing. How could she look so stern and still be so beautiful? I guessed that was all a part of her success.

The lieutenant man joined in the laughter. "Well, William, fancy your editorial page if—"

"It seems to me the both of you have nothing to lose, either," Sally broke in. "After all, Sander, this is an election year for you, too, you know. And you, William, you *know* your wife has her own attorney. What does that mean when the wife of Seattle's most prominent publisher gets her own attorney? Do you think I asked you all here just to snicker at my guest?"

That quieted them. Sally got up and walked around the table toward me. She stood behind me, picked up my long white braid and stroked it gently. Strange? You best believe I felt strange. I didn't dare move.

"This hair could be spun gold and it wouldn't be more valuable," she continued. "Isn't that so, Emil?"

Ridenour dabbed at his lips and said, "In certain mythologies, yes, the hair of an albino is considered mystical. But, of course, scientifically . . ."

"You of all of us, Emil, shouldn't count on science for his fortune. Your fortune was made from the *lack* of science," Sally said. Then she turned to the others and asked, "Did any man here get his success scientifically?"

"Yes, in the mathematical science of one man equals one vote," the lieutenant man said, smiling toward Chief Daniels. "Or," he added with a wry smile, "in your case, Dunckie, one man equals *two* votes."

Everyone laughed except me and Sally. Sally because she was mad and me because I had no idea what was happening.

"Then fine," Sally said curtly. "Laugh away everyone's futures. I tell you, there are tough times ahead and you, dear ol' DAD, are about to lose your job. I need you in that job and so do the rest of you."

"So, what is it you want us to do?" Chief Daniels asked. "Pray?"

Sally then took a gentler tack. "Well, I know you boys find my odd beliefs a little difficult to understand, but really— what harm in simply touching this gorgeous hair?"

"Touching her hair? Is that all?" Chief Daniels asked. "Why didn't you say so? Sure, I'll play your little game. What do I have to lose?"

He reached toward me, but Sally stood between me and the police chief. "One hundred dollars," she said. She even held out her hand as though she expected him to pull out a roll of bills from his pocket.

You know what? That was what he did. He pulled out two fifty-dollar bills from his wallet. Sally stood aside and handed him my braid. He held it and looked down into my eyes. What could I do but look back? I didn't even know what sort of luck I was supposed to be giving him.

Then he thanked Sally for the evening. "I'm expecting big things for that money," he added. "In fact, for a hundred bucks I want a memento." He took a knife from the table and cut off a few strands from my braid. Then he took one of the fifties from Sally and handed it to me, adding, "If you're going into this business, miss, you'd better learn to take your share upfront." He popped open his pocket watch, placed the lock of hair inside, then closed it.

Well, the following Tuesday was recall election day in Seattle. Chief of Police Duncan A. Daniels, dear ol' DAD, received a landslide vote of confidence.

William, the newspaperman, wrote a tongue-in-cheek editorial. The headline was "The Art of Luck." He mentioned me, my "charming uniqueness," my magical queue of white hair and the small lock of it in Chief Daniels's watch.

It was my first review.

Intelligent people understood the editorial and laughed and went on with their lives, amused but not moved. Naturally, the recall election was rigged. Just as the first election had been. Everyone in Seattle knew that.

But other people, thousands of them, in a time when the world was at war and a plague called the Spanish influenza was covering the earth, wanted to believe and took the editorial seriously.

My career, as Countess Polanski had foretold, was launched. I don't think there was anything I could have done to stop it.

And, as I soon found out, there was a huge difference between being a sideshow freak and being a star.

26

From there the rest was fast, easy and satisfying. I imagine all overnight rises to fame are. By October I was a Seattle sensation. And all I really did was watch and allow it to happen.

Halbie taught me mind reading tricks and Sally provided me with a wonderful new wardrobe from her dressmakers in San Francisco. Squirl donned a business suit, cleaned up his language and became my manager, while Dr. Ridenour began his advertising campaign. Each one got a percentage of my earnings.

The tricks of the mind reading trade are really quite easy, and if I was a quick study, it was because Halbie was a kind teacher to both Squirl and me. In mind reading, you simply memorize certain words and phrases, certain speech patterns. Other mind readers also used facial and hand cues, but because of my poor eyesight, Halbie kept those tricks to a minimum; a stance or broad gesture, maybe a sneeze or a well-timed cough. The way it would work was

Squirl, as my assistant, would go out among the audience and ask someone if he could have a personal article, which he would place in a velvet pouch. Something like a watch, brooch, hankie or something most folks carry with them. Then he'd ask me questions about what the item was. He'd toss me certain clues—which were really cues—and then I'd know the gold watch the man had was inscribed or the hankie was scented with peppermint or the brooch was very old, therefore an heirloom. This would start us off. Then I'd say I was getting a mental picture and start off on something so vague, so "perhaps," that it could probably happen to anyone. For instance, someone in your family is about to be very sick (of course *everyone* knew someone who had influenza) or be in great danger—that of course would be the war in Europe. I'd just make things up as I went along. It was fun. Like building my own fairy tales—being a writer, sort of. And for this I'd get applause, respect and money. Lying had never been easier.

And I was really good at it.

Of course, the big payoff was toward the end of each show. I would get this strong, dramatic sense from someone in the audience. I'd sway a little, look alarmed, ask for the houselights to be raised. I'd pick out someone who looked like they could afford it. I'd lift my smoked glasses and let everyone gasp at my colorless, oscillating eyes. I'd stare at my target and tell them great harm was about to come upon them and they should do anything—everything—they could to avert it. I told them to see me backstage after the show for further help.

That cost big. They always ended by stroking my hair for luck and then talking Squirl into allowing a small snip to be taken off the end so that my goodwill would stay with them. Well, they *thought* it was my hair. Actually, it was bleached wig hair that we stuck on the very end with an elastic band. I always consented to the trimming and I never had anyone ask for their money back. No doubt, if folks put any store in my abilities to bring good luck, then I could also probably bring bad luck, if they crossed me.

It was late fall. The Indian summer weather was glorious. Very little rain, very little wind. Bold mountains on either side of Puget Sound reflected the sun, accenting the blue of the sky and the green of the hills.

Squirl never knocked when he entered my rooms now. Odd, but I think I resented it. These were *my* rooms, even though they were provided by his sister. I took to locking my door just to make him ask. Oh, I still loved him, of that you may be sure.

But once he came busting in just as I was slipping out of my nightgown and you better believe I was mad. Back home, Babe was always bursting in on me. I wanted my privacy—even from Squirl.

Things were changing in me, and both Squirl and I knew it.

Squirl was enjoying his percentage of me as well. He enjoyed his high life. He was now above riding a jitney streetcar or a nickel-snatcher ferry. He'd put money down on a roadster, which he drove like a tipsy gambler late for a high-stakes game. I'd always known he was a gambler—after all, in a fashion, that's how we met.

Trouble was, I didn't think Squirl did all that well in the city. Whereas he'd been a champion of the log ponds, the flume, the forests and maybe even the mountains, it seemed as though the city beat him down. Just the opposite of me. Although he looked grand and high-living on the outside, I knew he drank, and gambled far more than he earned. Even *I* knew there were drinkers and there were gamblers, but never good drinking gamblers. I also knew that men would come looking for him and he'd charm his way out of things. He was that—charming.

Sometime in late October he lost his roadster. I don't know if he gambled it away or if it was repossessed. Knowing Squirl, he could have used it to buy his way out of the draft.

One Saturday afternoon shortly thereafter I was resting in my room because it was the last day of the season. I'd already done three shows that day and we were going to offer two more that night. One, the very last show, was for special, invited guests only. People from Seattle's upper crust. It was a scheme Ridenour had cooked up. He thought—and I suppose he was right—that if only certain people in high places were invited, everyone in lower places would scramble to see the other shows *first*.

But it was clearly becoming winter and time to close for the season. Squirl had been pushing Ridenour to stay open all winter and I knew it was because he hadn't saved one dime to see him through.

I was reading the *Seattle Post-Intelligencer.* I still found reading the newspapers one of the most relaxing, take-me-away-from-it-all activities. I was stunned to read that my father's mill had finally gone on strike. I smiled at first, thinking, That serves you right, Red Hankins. I thought about Babe swinging an ax, my father running the mill all by himself, and I thought about the angry strikers. But strikes could get ugly, and I lost my smile. I remembered Babe's words:

"Loyalty don't have nothin' to do with nothin'." Guess she was right.

There was a noise at the door. Squirl. He tried the door, found it locked and impatiently said, "Hey, it's me, Cordy. Let me in."

"I'm resting," I said, putting the newspaper down.

"Come on. I'm in a jam."

"Oh, Squirl . . ."

"Do I have to get my key?"

I got out of bed and opened the door for him. As cranky as I was, tired, too, my heart still thudded when I saw him. He grinned at me, kissed me on the cheek as he passed and made himself at home in my sitting room.

"I need to get some rest, Squirl," I said. "What do you need?"

"Your John Hancock," he said, pulling out some papers.

"What for?"

"Ridenour won't let me draw my take for tonight's show until you sign for it. He says it's *your* money and you should decide who gets theirs and when. How do you like that? That toad-eating quack telling *me* that? Sometimes I think he forgets who's responsible for all this good fortune in the first place."

The faint light danced on his beautiful face and, even pouting, he was masculine and thrilling and full of promise.

"You and me still planning on sailing to the South Seas someday?" I asked, changing the subject. "Remember, Squirl? Copra and all. By the way, what's copra?" I sat down next to him and took his hand.

He looked at me, kissed me on the lips this time and answered, "You're copra. You're also gold, silver and my lucky charm."

He handed me the voucher to sign. I set it down.

"What if I don't sign that?"

"Then I'd forge your signature, like I did the last three times you gave me an advance," he replied, pulling out a silver cigarette case.

"So why'd you come asking this time?" I asked.

"Well, I might need a little more than tonight's advance," he admitted, lighting his cigarette.

"You really aren't a very good poker player, are you, Squirl?"

"You sound just like Sally. You know, that's what I don't like about you livin' here, Cordy. I think you two women sit around, compare notes and rip me to shreds. Hell, that's why I left home as young as I did. Her and our ol' lady always goin' against me."

"You know how I feel about you, Squirl," I said.

"So, how you fixed for cash?" he asked, squeezing my hand.

I had every dime I'd made, some in my top drawer, some hidden elsewhere. "How much you need?" I walked to the drawer and pulled out a box.

"Seventy-five, if you can manage it," he said.

To be cute, I handed him three quarters and said, "Here, sonny. And buy yourself a candied apple."

But Squirl didn't laugh. In fact, his face went very cold. He held out his hand, snapped his fingers and said, "Very funny, Fanny Brice. Seventy-five *dollars*, Cordy. And don't tell me you can't spare it."

I handed him the bills and asked, "Ever read Aesop?"

"Yeah, yeah. I know—'The Grasshopper and the Ant.' If I had a sawbuck for every time Sally's told me that one, I wouldn't need to borrow money."

"So then you know which bug you are," I said, closing my drawer.

He pocketed the bills and the three quarters, kissed me and said, "Well, lucky for me you're not only an ant, but you're the whole damn colony. Thanks. I'll pay you back."

The phone rang. It was Gina, saying Sally wanted to know if I had her blue velvet slippers. I said yes, come on up and I'd have them for her. I went to my closet and rummaged around the floor until I found both slippers. Finding matching shoes had certainly been easier when I only had three pairs back home in Centner's Mill.

I returned with them about the time Gina knocked at my door. I handed them out and just as I did, Squirl came over and said, "I'll let you take your nap. Look, I'll be runnin' errands, so I'll just meet you before the first show." Another peck on my cheek and he left, saying he'd planned a humdinger show for all the muckety-mucks that night and to wear something special.

I locked the door and looked around my room. Squirl had stolen from me before—little things mostly. We both knew that we both knew it.

I opened my dresser drawer to count the damage this time. Naturally, I kept my big money well hidden deep in my closet. But most of my small money was there. I think he took only another twenty or so. I couldn't even be sure of that. I didn't keep good records, but thought maybe this would be a good time to start a bank account.

Out of curiosity, I rummaged deeper. Sally had loaned me several pieces of jewelry. I'd kill Squirl if he'd taken something entrusted to me. I could tell from the mess that he'd been rummaging also.

I looked way in the back where I kept my very most secret

things—the letters to my father I'd written but never sent, my best sketches, some photographs and newspaper clippings about me. And the old article about Babe that I'd stolen from Ridenour's pickling room closet when I'd first arrived.

Odd, that was the only thing missing. The article about Giganta—still wanted for murder and with a ten thousand-dollar reward for her capture.

Oh God, why had I kept that thing?

27

I will tell you one thing I've come to learn: People are different in the city. At first I thought the differences were charming—little eccentric things that all those city cousin and country cousin jokes come from. But you stay around long enough and you'll see less charm and more harm. I don't want to say evil, because there are a lot of fine folks living in the city—city born, city bred. But there's also a sinister side. Maybe it was just the side of Seattle I'd chosen to live on and the people whom I was forced to build my trust in.

They probably saw the likes of me coming for a country mile. And maybe they saw charming differences in me also—outside of those differences that are ever so apparent. Beyond that, there's my so-called innocence, or, if you ask me, my downright stupidity. You can rely on that innocent angle for only so long. Then you have to smarten up.

I'd given up on getting any rest and decided to go over early to prepare for the two shows I was scheduled to give that last evening. I also wanted to think over what Squirl might be up to.

I had been given a set of rooms in the medical museum as my dressing rooms, and they also served as an office for "private consultations," which Ridenour thought I might have to start making during the off-season. Not so much for the money, he said, but to keep my valuable name "out and about." No one but me had their own room in the museum, but I don't think any of the other acts resented it.

I was setting out my Oriental silk dress, as the afternoon shows were ending. The folks from the Ten in Ones—the sideshows—were gathering in the medical museum to hand over their receipt bags to Ridenour.

Outside I could hear Halbie talking about how little money he had made this season now that I was the big hit and he hoped to God I remembered him kindly when I grew old and wrote my memoirs.

"Look, Halbie," someone said, "that little white monkey's bringing in more folks than we've had around here since we opened. Besides, the way I hear it, you're getting a nice little take of her."

I listened at my door. I heard someone say if I was smart I'd head south with Halbie for the winter and get away from this place.

Then I heard Carlotta say, "That girl is nothing more'n a cheap bally-act. All velvet today—washed-out burlap tomorrow. By this time next year she'll be the second-rate act in a third-rate carnie. Once the novelty of her wears off."

"Say, when did the novelty of *you* wear off, you little freak?" someone asked.

They all laughed.

"I'm no more a freak'n the rest of you!"

They laughed even harder. Someone said, "Oh, I don't know about that."

"I'm a licensed nurse, I'll have you know!"

"Yeah, drummed out of the profession just like Ridenour. If we're freaks, you're both quacks!" Another performer had jumped in.

"Look at that, she even walks like a quacker! Quack! Quack!" the man called out after her.

It was a reflex action. Those two words, "little freak," ran through me, and something from my past made me jump up, open the door and say to Carlotta's tormentors, "Stop it! All of you! Just stop it!"

Carlotta, as I somehow knew she would, looked up at me and said, "I can fight my own battles."

I looked around at my fellow freaks and said, "Carlotta *is* a nurse. I've seen her license." They all looked at me like I was insane, defending Carlotta.

Then I said down to Carlotta, "I've smashed my finger in a drawer. Could you come and look at it?" I turned and went back into my room. Although I didn't see it, I knew Carlotta was giving them a superior "So there!" with her eyes. She followed me in and asked which finger. I showed her one. Of course, it was fine, but I winced when she wiggled it.

"Ice it now. Ice it after the show," she said flatly.

She turned to leave. Then she stopped and added, without looking at me, "It'll be good as the other nine come morning. You know, I *did* have a license. Was a nurse in an orphanage back in Chicago. Once. That was a long time ago."

I remembered Carlotta the Dancing Dwarf standing next to Babe in the photograph.

"So, how long have you been with Ridenour? I mean, how did you . . . ?"

Carlotta and I had shared maybe three civil sentences since that first day in the museum basement. Here, in the soft gaslight of my dressing room, I saw she wasn't as grotesque—her eyes maybe weren't as cold—as I'd thought.

"It don't work, the likes of us trying to be normal folk. Sure, I got my nurse's license. Got my pin. Got my cap, too. Even got a job. Something goes wrong, the freak's the first one to go."

Was she actually inviting me into her past? A past that included Babe?

"What went wrong?"

"One of the unwed mothers we took in was scared seeing me one day. Then her babies was born Siamese. You know what that is?" She walked to my closet and fingered the various gowns hanging there.

"Stuck together?"

"Stuck's the word. Stuck's the *perfect* word. Babies died. Blessing, of course. Ridenour heard about the babies. Come lookin' for 'em. So I sold him the babies for his sideshow. They was sackin' me anyhow. The four of us have been together ever since. They're downstairs. Been meaning to change their formaldehyde for some time now."

"Bet you've met a lot of people, traveling the country and all." How could I get onto the subject of Giganta without Carlotta's getting suspicious? "Made some friends."

"Hard to make good friends when you travel so much." Then, for the first time ever, I saw Carlotta smile. "Hard to look at me and believe my best friend ever was a giant."

"A giant?"

"Good ol' Fern. Saved my life once. She's dead now. Just as well. Anyhow, Ridenour got tired of the road. He's got connections here in Seattle. Here I am—his assistant. Worked my way up from shill. Closest thing to nursin' I'll ever get. Shovin' smellin' salts under noses of weak-kneed fainters. Then tendin' to one of Sally's stupid girls when they mess up. I could go to jail for a million years for the things I've done for Emil Ridenour. They'd *hang* him."

She stopped, turned and looked as though she'd already told me too much. "Anyhow, thanks for . . ." She tilted her head toward the door, smiled and left.

The silence of the empty museum was always a big, frightening silence to me. So the knock on my door a few minutes later startled me. I opened it, saying, "Squirl, I need to talk . . ."

But it wasn't Squirl. It was Carlotta again. She'd brought me some ice. She said nothing, just handed it up to me through the half-open door. I thanked her and watched her walk back down the hall until she disappeared into the eerie darkness.

28

Squirl didn't show up for the first show. I knew he had pressing debts to pay, so I didn't think much about it. Ridenour did, though. He asked me backstage where the devil that Squirl was. I lied. I said Squirl had business back in town. Ridenour's reply to that was odd. He said every woman he ever knew who lied for her man ended up either broke, broken-down or just dead. Then he patted my cheek and went out onstage.

When Squirl missed a show Ridenour went on as my assistant. I always hated working with him. He was vain and kept trying to push the medical museum if I even so much as suggested someone had a medical complaint. Out of spite, I insisted this one poor fool was coughing because of a psychological ailment and that using the I Ching would point the way.

We had an hour break between shows. This last "invitation only" show was really important for all of us. These were the big spenders of Seattle. Looking out over the audience, I could see the glittering of diamonds, smell the Paris perfumes and the faint scent of mothballs from the tuxedos, hear the giddy talk of those who'd had too much champagne at the dinner Sally had provided. I was peeping out at the crowd from backstage, wondering why I should be more nervous in front of this group than any other. If anything, the fact that they had probably all been drinking Canadian wine and breaking the law should have made me feel as though I had something over them. I tried to think of a way to put that into my act. But I thought twice when I saw Chief of Police Duncan Daniels was front row center and probably the tipsiest one in the crowd. Sally sat prominently next to him. She seldom came to my performances but had said she wouldn't miss this one for anything.

Inspecting the crowds before my shows was a habit. I'd peep through the side curtain, wondering if someday I'd look out and see my father or Babe there. Babe especially was on my mind that night. I was still cursing myself for not destroying that article. The worst part, though, was my own evil reason for not destroying it. I remembered my wicked fantasy of chasing Babe out of the woods and watching her hang and running the reward money under my father's nose. Well, that fantasy had died a guilty death. Maybe it was because I was growing up.

It was two minutes to curtain and Squirl still wasn't anywhere around. Ridenour was in the opposite wing, glaring at me. I saw him purposefully bring out his pocket watch, look at it and snap it shut.

The overturning of some sets backstage announced Squirl's arrival. He was pulling on his tuxedo coat as he ran toward me. He came up, slicked back his hair and kissed me. Dr. Ridenour had seen him and was out introducing the act.

"Where have you been?" I asked him, drawing back from the smell of cigars and whiskey.

"Seattle. Doin' business," he said. "Here, help me with this."

I fixed his tie and asked, "What sort of business?"

He grinned down at me and replied, "Business that's gonna make us both rich."

Ridenour was finishing up his announcement.

"And now, ladies and gentlemen, for your mystical pleasure, I present Cordelia, Daughter of the Orient, Seer of All Sights. And, as her guide through the Portals of Perception, Burleson."

Squirl had borrowed Sally's father's name—Burleson—for the act. None of us had thought Squirl was a suitable name for my tuxedo-clad, handsome and, tonight, quite drunk assistant. Ridenour then asked to have the stage lights lowered because of the delicacy of my eyes. The lighting man had a way of pinking out the light, and I'd been told I looked very beautiful on the stage, in my silks, in that light. Of course, the pink on pink of my eyes was always a bit startling to the crowd. I'd come to anticipate and adore that first "oooohhhh" when the lights came up on me. But even the low stage lights hurt, and Ridenour would bow to me and place my smoked glasses on me, bow again and then back offstage.

I gave the audience a bow of respect. The violin and piano musicians played something Oriental until Squirl came out onstage and explained he would be going out among them and, once the room was silent, the readings could begin. Of course, most people already knew about my act, either from the publicity or from word-of-mouth.

I would sit on a chair like a throne, my long dress gathered around me. Squirl by then would have targeted the first person in the audience who wanted a reading. Squirl would ask his or her name, turn his back to me, put a personal effect into a silk pouch, draw the strings tight and then hold it up for me. Based on what he said, I would tell him what was hidden in the pouch. In the case of the first person this evening, it was a cigarette case. Almost always the first person was a cigarette case.

We started out easy. From there, though, I got a "message," put my hand to my head and said, "Wait."

"Quiet, please, good ladies and gentlemen."

"The cigarette case is . . . stolen."

The audience reacted appropriately and looked over to the man, who, of course, looked very insulted. Then I added, "No—yes. Yes, that is not *your* cigarette case, sir."

"Sir, is this your cigarette case?" Squirl asked as he pulled the silver case out of the pouch and held it up for the crowd to see.

The man looked at it, turned it over and looked at the inscription and then, embarrassed, told the crowd he must have picked up his friend's case during dinner. Indeed, it wasn't his case.

The crowd applauded and I just bowed my head.

How did I know? Squirl, of course, had asked the gentleman's name, looked at the cigarette case and had noticed that the inscription didn't jibe. So he gave me the bonus clue of "good." Any time he used that word, it meant he thought the article might not belong to the person who had given it to him. We had a hundred clues to lead us anywhere we wanted. Sometimes it was a game between Squirl and me what we would reveal to people about themselves. We were right about nine out of ten times. The tenth time? Cosmic forces usually took the blame.

We did a few more readings, saving some of the best for last. Squirl and I had perfected some routines that usually set the audience clapping. We really did work well together. I had noticed Halbie standing discreetly at the back of the theater. He was wearing his black organdy dress, which he only wore on special occasions, and I was honored.

A woman elegantly dressed in white fur stood up and motioned for Squirl to call on her next. I watched Squirl approach her. She was loud and drunk and usually we avoided those types. But she was insistent and she pulled Squirl to her side. Then I saw Halbie broadly motion to me, as though to catch my attention. I stepped out of the lights and tried not to squint at him, but he was definitely trying to tell me something. He puffed out his chest, then crossed his arms like a disapproving schoolmarm.

The woman turned her back and I focused back down at Squirl, then back at Halbie. Squirl looked expressionless and now Halbie ventured a little out of the shadows so I could see him better. I had no idea what our mark could have possibly placed in the pouch, but obviously Halbie did. The woman swayed as she stood in her tiny heels. Then she whispered something in Squirl's ear.

"A . . . ," Squirl began, grinning a little. "Cordelia, Daughter of the Orient, this lovely lady has given me a personal article for your consideration."

I ran through the clue words and had no idea where Squirl was leading me with this. Halbie knew my sight wasn't the best, but he was a master of broad, theatrical movement. When he motioned to his face, I thought to answer . . .

"Something round."

Halbie nodded, then put his wrist to his ear, as though to daintily adjust his elegant coif.

"A wristwatch?" I asked, hoping it didn't sound like I was asking Halbie. Women didn't use wristwatches. That couldn't be right. Squirl could have easily given me a watch clue. All he had to say was "eyes," as in "watch" this.

Squirl said, "Yes, Cordelia. A watch it is. Now we have time for . . ."

But Halbie was now standing with his hands on his hips . . . another obvious motion to get my attention. Then he pointed to Squirl. I knew he was mouthing a word, but his face was just a shadowed blur. Still, it was the last show and I was feeling a little bold and giddy myself. I stepped closer to the edge of the stage and looked at the fur-clad woman clinging to Squirl and said, "I'm getting something else. Burleson?" Halbie nodded and smiled and ticked his head toward Squirl while he rolled up his feminine organdy sleeve to look at his masculine watch. What would that woman be doing with Squirl's watch? My face turned cold and I asked for the houselights to be raised. I removed my glasses. Halbie returned to the shadows. The crowd hushed as I said, "Ladies and gentlemen, the watch apparently belongs to my good assistant, Burleson."

Squirl's face was as blank as I had ever seen it. The woman put her hands to her astonished, flushed face and said I was right. I felt sick to my stomach as she threw her arms around him.

"I suppose how the watch came into your possession is strictly between the two of you," I said, trying to sound glib and sophisticated.

The audience roared, Halbie clapped wildly and Squirl glared back at me as he located our last mark. He was a handsome young soldier and I invited him to come back to my dressing room in the medical museum for a personal reading. He was a flier and I flirted with him a little to see how Squirl would react.

With that, the show ended. I took my accolades, and the season was over. I walked with the soldier back to the museum, where, with Squirl glowering at me, I gave the flier a private consultation.

I allowed him a small snip of my hair. Only I snipped it off myself so that I knew it was truly part of my braid and not from the bleached wig Squirl usually snipped from.

I wished him Godspeed and said he would return soon and in victory. I wouldn't let Squirl charge him anything.

"I happen to know that flyboy was worth at least twenty bucks!" Squirl snapped after he'd left.

"I couldn't take his money. He's going to need every cent of it," I said.

"Oh, so now you're takin' yourself seriously, huh?" Squirl said, loosening his tie and lighting a cigarette. "That would be a big mistake, Cordelia, Daughter of the Orient. Remember, this is just entertainment."

"Oh? Then how do you think I knew about that floozie having *your* watch?" I challenged.

Squirl must have been sobering up. He looked at me, studying my face. "Just how *did* you know that?" he asked suspiciously.

"I think the question here is what was that woman doing with *your watch?*"

"You're the damn clairvoyant. You tell me!"

I turned my back on him and started to undo my braid and brush my hair.

Squirl watched me for a moment, then took my brush and started brushing my hair for me. It was paradise. Long strokes, gentle strokes. He said, "Cordy, you *know* I've had some money problems. But let's not fight. Not when things are changin' for the better."

I looked at him in the mirror. "So who was that lush?"

"That lush was *Mrs.* Cecil Armory. Her husband is my pawnbroker."

Yes, that made perfect sense. I even wondered what little articles of *mine* Mrs. Cecil Armory wore. Articles. Article—Babe. In my jealousy, I'd almost forgotten. I wondered if I should just come out and ask Squirl about the Giganta article.

He brushed my hair in silence, laying long locks gently down my back. "I just hate to see you take yourself—all of this—so seriously," he said.

"I'm not taking myself seriously, Squirl," I said. "But taking that soldier's money would have been wrong. I don't know why, I just know it's wrong."

"That's what people expect when they come to see you. Besides, we need all we can get."

"We do?" I asked.

"Doesn't everybody?" he asked back.

I was pulling hair out of my brush and was ready to throw it away when Squirl grabbed it from me. "Hey, that's like spun gold, Cordy. I can sell this stuff."

I turned and looked at him. "Is that why my hairbrushes are always so clean at home?" I asked. I kept my brushes in my top dresser drawer—where I kept my money, where I *had* kept that article on Babe.

He kissed my cheek and said, "You're my little gold mine."

"So tell me more about this business deal you're working on to make us all rich."

"Still ironin' out the details." He was now lounging on my couch.

There was a knock and Halbie leaned his head in. "Hi, kids. What's doing? Great show, Cordy." He pulled a bottle of whiskey out of his huge, deep pockets. "Hi, Squirl. Want a belt to celebrate the end of the season?"

Of course he did.

I'm not saying I was taking my so-called mind reading talents seriously. I'm not saying I possessed even a smidgen of woman's intuition. But I am saying that something—way down deep inside of me—began to ache. It's hard to explain. I was hurting and I had no idea why.

29

I watched Halbie and Squirl pass the bottle a few times. I wished I'd told Halbie I was tired and just wanted to go home, because I wanted to talk to Squirl some more. In private. And this time about Babe.

Turned out, it was Squirl who brought it up.

It hadn't taken too much liquor to get Squirl talking about how we could, all three of us, if we played our cards just right, become rich overnight.

"How so? Kidnap John Wilkes Booth and hold him for ransom? Never work. Ridenour'll just order another one," Halbie said. He'd taken his wig off and that was the first time I'd ever seen him without it. I was surprised to see that he was nearly bald, making him a much older man than he was a woman.

"Nope. Halbie, why don't you ask Cordy about her stepmother?" Squirl grinned at me. He cocked his jaw the same way he had when he dared me down that flume.

So he was going to come right out with it.

Halbie touched my hand and said, only half mocking, "Oh, my poor dear. Is she a wicked stepmother?"

Squirl put his feet up on the table, balanced his chair on the back legs and folded his arms. "Well?" he asked, still grinning at me.

Why play the game? I thought.

"My stepmother is wanted for murder," I said to Halbie. Then I looked right at Squirl and added, "There's a ten-thousand-dollar reward for her."

"You're *almost* right," Squirl said, taking the article out of his tuxedo coat pocket. "In case you were wonderin' why I was late tonight, I was visitin' the Seattle police. They called Chicago for me. Seems the reward has been in a trust account since 1907, and with interest is now valued at thirteen thousand dollars." He placed the article on the table. "And some change."

Halbie picked up the article, pulled out a pair of glasses, put them on and read it. I knew by his expression, how his mouth dropped open, that he knew about Babe, or rather, Giganta.

"I don't get it," Halbie said. "Are you saying Giganta is still alive and she's . . . *your* stepmother?"

"Small world, ain't it?" Squirl said, bringing his chair back up.

"Especially for someone her size," Halbie muttered, looking down at the article.

"And she's a real peach, ain't she, Cordy? Tell Halbie some of the stories you told me. I know! Tell him what was left of that logger after she . . ."

Sure, I had a thousand stories about Babe, any number of

which might have ended in someone's death, but I silenced Squirl and said to Halbie, "Tell me what you know about her."

He hesitated, glancing at Squirl.

"Well, like that article says, I heard she was wanted for killing her husband. Oh, you talk about your rotten peaches! His name was Ebenezer Somebody. Fancied himself an impresario. We all knew he was just a poor man's Barnum." He leaned into us and whispered, "Like someone else we all know." Then he sat back and added, "Anyway, supposedly she killed him and escaped into Lake Michigan, where she was presumed drowned. Squirl, did the police tell you who was offering the reward?"

"No, the Chicago boys said that was confidential," Squirl answered.

"Well, confidentially," Halbie continued, now whispering, "if you want your thirteen thousand dollars, just walk down that hall and knock on Ridenour's door."

"Why?" both Squirl and I asked.

"Because it's *his* money," Halbie replied, just barely mouthing the words.

"Ridenour put up the reward? Why?" I asked.

Halbie motioned us in closer and replied, "Because she was married to his partner and it was him she killed. Or so they said."

"Partner?" Squirl asked.

"No fooling, kids. Emil and Ebenezer's World of the Absurd. Just a two-bit carnie act. They used to follow the big boys around, town to town. Set up a mile away. They booked the acts that couldn't make the big time.

"This was years ago," Halbie continued. "Who *really* knew what happened but Ridenour and Giganta? Let me see, I was playing someplace in New Jersey. Had me a magic act back then. Well, everyone in show business knew about Giganta. God, she was *huge*. Stronger'n any man I ever saw. In fact, some folks thought she *was* a man. But I'll tell you, she was all woman and heaven help the man who thought otherwise. You know, I once saw her in a tug-of-war with one of the Barnum and Bailey elephants. It was just a small elephant, but guess who won."

"She did, of course," I said. I'd seen her bring Meg the mule to her knees without so much as a heave-ho. All it took was her scowl. "What else do you know?"

"Well, her temper was legendary." Halbie stood up, went to the door, opened it and made sure there was no one in the hallway, listening. "The gossip on the carnie circuit was she killed him in a fit of anger. Some said she was drunk. Some said she did it in self-defense. Then I heard others say Giganta was fiercely loyal to the other performers. She was always coming to their aid, especially—guess who." He tapped Carlotta's small face in the photograph. "Our very own, very charming Carlotta. Well, who knows anything? Gossip's never hotter'n when it's riding through a carnie. I've just heard it said that no matter what else Giganta was, she always defended the defenseless," Halbie concluded. A wistful smile came across his face as he added, "Wish she'd been with me that time in Boston."

Squirl looked at me. "But she *is* a demon, isn't she, Cordy? She even threatened my life. Remember, Cordy?"

"What else?" I asked Halbie.

"Well, every now and then I'd hear from one of my cronies that Giganta was seen cooking in Mexico, cutting cane in Cuba, then logging down in Oregon. Rumors. A woman like that just naturally gives rumors a reason to be. All I know is, the mention of Giganta around here is forbidden. Ridenour says he doesn't want to ever hear that woman's name again." Halbie looked at me and added, "I'm sorry to be talking about your stepmother so. It's really not very nice of me."

"Don't worry, Halbie. You ain't tellin' her nothin' she don't already know. Huh, Cordy?" Squirl said eagerly.

I didn't answer. I wished then I *could* read minds. "So, Giganta didn't drown after all," Halbie said. "Good. I was always pulling for her. Everyone know's Ridenour was practically a slave owner back then. He'd just gotten kicked out of medical school. So don't let anyone ever tell you he's a real doctor, because he's not."

But Squirl seemed far beyond old gossip. Pointing to the photograph on the table, he said, "Listen, Ridenour can't know anything about this. If he finds out we know where Giganta is, he'll bring her out on his own. Why pay us for something he can do himself?"

"Well, if the gossip I've heard is true, Ridenour keeps that reward open for one reason and one reason only," Halbie said. "As long as there's money on her head, she'll stay well away. Why do you suppose that is?"

When we didn't answer, he went on, "Because some people think maybe Giganta *knows* something. Ridenour keeps money on Giganta and Giganta keeps hidden away and quiet. Oh, but talk about the event of the century. Wouldn't you love to sell tickets if those two was ever to meet up?"

Halbie again realized he was speaking about my stepmother. "Oh, Cordy, you must think I'm awful. Spreading gossip like this and talking about her like . . . I'm sorry. I'm sure Giganta can't help it, the way she is. Like all of us."

I finally had to speak up. "I don't care what they say and I don't care about gossip. We can't turn her in, Squirl."

"What do you mean we can't? Of course we can and we're gonna. Don't be stupid, Cordy. You have no love lost for her. I've heard you go on and on about how you hate her, how she nearly drowned you once, how drunk she gets four times a year and you havin' to clean up her puke. You got a right to hate her. Of course you can do this."

"And I can't do this to my father," I added.

"Oh, there's another lovin' relationship. Go ahead and tell Halbie how much you love your father."

I looked at Halbie and wondered if, after all his years of fortune-telling, he could read my expression. Could my face tell him something I myself didn't know?

Squirl grabbed my arm and said, "Cordy. This could be our ticket to the world. The South Seas, South America, South Anywhere in the World. With this kind of money the three of us can hop a freighter, be in the South Seas by Christmas and put together our own show."

"Oh, that would be paradise," Halbie said, pouring another drink. "I've always wanted to hop a freighter and just go."

"No," I said. "Look, I don't care how much I hate them, I just can't do it. It's wrong, okay? It's blood money."

"Oh yeah? Well, look at it this way: Sooner or later someone's gonna find that woman. Might as well be us as anyone else. Think of the years of torment that beast's put on you," Squirl said, his voice so cool, so convincing, that I forgot his words.

"And besides, maybe she's not guilty," Squirl continued, walking around the room, almost pacing. "Just because we're gonna bring her in don't mean she's gonna hang or nothing.

Maybe that man just slipped or something and hit his head. Or maybe *he* did it." He pointed toward Ridenour's office. "Maybe even Carlotta. You know, they've been together a long time."

"Yes," Halbie added, "then we'd actually be helping to solve a crime. Maybe get her name cleared."

"Yeah. And wouldn't it be great to pry that kind of money out of Ridenour after all the puny wages he's been shellin' out?"

"I won't be a part of this and neither will you," I said with all the authority I could put in my voice.

Squirl pulled me up to his chest. He put his arms around me and said, "Cordy, this is for *us*. You know I have money problems right now. How can I ask you to marry me without the money to keep you the way you deserve? What could I offer you without money? We'd just end up driftin' from one loggin' camp to another. I'd walk logs and you'd probably cook for a camp full of smelly, foulmouthed loggers. That is, if we could even *find* the work. You know how far Red Hankins's word carries."

Did he say marry?

"But it's wrong, Squirl," I whispered up to him.

"Do you really want to go back to that kind of life?"

Halbie, uncomfortable, got up and said, "I can see you two kids have plans to make. Cordy, this is your kin. I won't be a part of this if you say so."

"I have to think," I said.

Squirl brought my face around to his and added, "And how fast did your *kin* come runnin' to find you when you ran off, Cordy? It ain't as though a girl like you just blends in anywhere. If they wanted, they could have found you. So while you're thinkin', think on that."

There it was. In clear, concise words—Squirl had just diagnosed that unknown pain in my gut. Then it occurred to me: The only thing worse than a girl running away was when nobody cared enough to even come looking. Suicide note or not.

"Well, you let me know," Halbie said, his voice soft and kind. "No matter what, I want you to think about getting out of town, Cordy. Come with the Ten in One south for the winter. It'll do you good to get away from all this mess."

"She's not goin' anywhere but with me, Halbie," Squirl said. He tightened his arm around my waist and held me close to him. "We're a team."

30

I wanted to walk home alone that night, but Squirl insisted on escorting me. How had it all become so crisscrossed? How many nights had I dreamt Squirl and I would marry? Run away together? Was it really about to come true?

Squirl was almost like a little boy on our walk home. Yes, I knew he'd been drinking and sometimes that made him do crazy things. On the boardwalk he walked for a distance on his hands. Then he walked on the edge of the handrail like a high-wire walker.

"Why don't you come down from there before you fall off and drown? Half of that reward money is a lot more than a third," I said.

He jumped down and took me by the shoulders. "Wow. Just what I was thinkin'. You know, Cordy, I think that's why you and me're gonna be so good together. We think alike."

I recognized the glint in his eye. "Like?"

"Like why split the reward three ways when we can have it all?" he asked.

"Cut out Halbie? But if it weren't for Halbie . . . ," I began. But Squirl wasn't listening, so I stopped and pulled him back. "Hey. I thought you two were friends."

"Oh, we are. We are. Halbie's a terrific . . . guy," Squirl said, smiling down at me.

"But we talked about maybe taking that money and the three of us starting a new act someplace else."

Squirl seemed to have an answer for everything. "Cordy, the important thing is you and me. With that kind of money you and me can go *anywhere*, write our own ticket . . ."

"Squirl, how much money do you owe?" It was the first time I'd ever spoken harshly to him.

"Enough to look for opportunity and not enough for you to worry about."

"How much?"

Squirl pulled me around by the arm and kissed me. In between his kisses, he whispered, "You belong to me, Cordelia. Tell me you'll marry me and you'll do as I say."

"I've loved you forever," I whispered, "but . . ."

He wrapped his arms around me and said, "But nothing. I've been wantin' to take you away from here for a long time. Now it's possible."

"I just don't know if I can do it."

"Okay, you got doubts," he said, his voice not velvety anymore but rational and slow.

"Oh, not about us. About Babe."

"Fine. Tell you what. We won't do this if you don't want to."

"I just—"

"Nope. Not unless you're one hundred percent sure."

We started walking again, slower and not touching.

"Can I sleep on it?" I asked.

"Yes, do that, Cordy. But while you're sleepin', do some dreamin' about you and me, huh?"

We walked back toward Sally's. Squirl talked about all the grand things we could do with that kind of money. He failed to mention *how* we were going to get that money. He just said he was working on a plan and it was going to be easy as pie, which was odd—"easy as pie" was one of Babe's favorite expressions.

We came around the corner of Cousin Sally's. Simon was leaning against the building. He looked over and saw us kiss good night. Squirl ran off saying he'd forgotten something back in the park.

He called out, "First thing in the morning, I want your answer."

I waved goodbye, but he was gone.

I looked at Simon and we both knew there was probably a crap game waiting for Squirl somewhere.

Two finely dressed gentlemen came out; Simon tipped his hat to them and signaled for a taxi to come over. One of the men, drunk I think, saw me and stumbled over to me to touch my hair. I was beginning to hate that. Simon got to him, tossed him gently into the taxi and said, "See you gentlemen sometime soon." And he signaled for the driver to leave.

Simon looked at me and said, a little fatherishly, "You best take to wearing your cap once again, Miss Cordy. You and that hair of yours gets any more famous and someday you're going to wake up bald."

I laughed and said that would probably serve me right.

"You mind me giving you some advice, Miss Cordy?" he asked.

Here it comes, I thought. Simon never once pretended to like Squirl.

"No, of course not."

"Then you listen to me. You got yourself a nice little thing going for you here. Folks pay you good money and everyone respects good money. Squirl's got nothing but bad money. Oh, it may come to him good, but money spends some time in Squirl's pocket and it plain turns bad. Forget all about that Squirl."

I looked up into his huge black eyes and simply said, "I can't."

He opened the door for me and I went inside.

I went straight to my room. It was chilly and Gina had lit a fire, which seemed to crackle a "welcome home" to me. Funny, even as a kid back at Centner's Mill, I'd find that gazing into dancing flames helped me think.

I sank into a chair and I think I stayed there, listening, staring, thinking, for an hour. I didn't give a tinker's dam about Babe, so why was I so bothered that Squirl—in an effort to secure our future—was going to bring her in? In a way, maybe he was right. Maybe I *had* earned that money . . . hourly wages paid in full for the years of work and the fear and the misery. So, I'd have money and Babe would have what? Justice?

Cinderella. Why Cinderella popped into my mind just then, I don't know. I couldn't help smiling into the embers. In a way, I was Cinderella—I'd been to the ball and found my prince. Now I was sitting safely in the palace, my prince off raiding kingdoms, but with my wicked stepmother still a problem. What *did* become of Cinderella's stepmother? My smile slowly disappeared as I stared into the flames. I wasn't Cinderella and this wasn't a fairy tale. This was real life.

The fact that Babe was married to my father didn't make her any less a murderess. The fact that no one knew but a handful of us carnival freaks didn't make it any less a crime. What if Babe *had* killed her husband? No one knew the cold stare, the hard face, the brutal strength more than me. Could she? Yes, she could.

But could I? Me turning in a murderess, in a way, turned me into a murderess too.

Then I thought of *him*. My father. God, what would he say if he knew about Giganta? Had she told him? No, she'd never told him. My father never would have tolerated a murderess in his house. I'd seen him arrest thieves, run cheaters out of camp. I'd seen him watch and do nothing when a group of angry loggers tarred and feathered a man who didn't pay off a gambling debt. He'd never tolerate dishonesty, let alone murder. No, she'd never told him. Maybe I'd be doing him a favor if we brought her in. Keeping the Red Hankins Code of Justice sparkly clean.

Brought her in? What was I thinking? Squirl was clever and beguiling. At times I thought he could charm the clouds right out of the sky, but the idea that he and he alone could bring Babe down off that mountain was almost funny. With most of our military troops overseas, exactly which army was going to back him up?

I must have been exhausted. Why else was I laughing out loud? Was it because even though I hated and feared Babe for her strength and temper, I somehow admired her too? Sort of like an old-growth fir—solid, strong and stubborn—you know it's not going anywhere until you just cut it down and even then it'll give you a fight.

Stop it, Cordy! I told myself. But I couldn't stop. Too many unanswered questions. I actually thought about going home to find the answers. Get to the bottom of the whole thing. Of course, if Babe could kill a man she could kill a girl. And if she'd gone to God knows what lengths to keep her true identity a secret, one more little murder—mine—wouldn't matter much.

As Babe herself had so often grumbled, "In for a dime, in for a dollar."

31

I didn't get much sleep that night, and most of what I did get was in the large chair in front of my fireplace. Sometime toward morning, I'd wandered into my bed, and when I woke up I was angry at myself for sleeping in my dress. I'd done that once at home and I'd thought Babe was going to shoot me for it. She'd said I could damn well spend the morning trying to iron out those wrinkles myself. I did, and she was right. It took forever and I learned my lesson.

But all I had to do now was to hand that dress to Gina and tell her when I wanted it back, go to my closet, close my eyes and pull out another dress.

I soaked in the bathtub and started to go over the events of the previous evening. I looked at the fingers on my left hand and imagined a wedding ring—a large diamond—right there. I whispered, "Mrs. Cordelia Burleson." Then I thought how wonderful it was that Sally and I would be sisters.

Sally. I didn't think she was going to be happy about this.

One more reason for Squirl and me to run away, of course, but I'd rather get married with her blessing.

A runaway. That's what I'd been when I came to Seattle and now that's what I was going to be leaving it. So much for improvement. Except I was going to run away with Squirl and with a trunk full of money.

I heard my mantel clock strike ten and thought I should probably hurry. I had to find Squirl and give him my answer, which would be: Yes, I would marry him and yes, my dowry would be Babe.

I hated to admit that I could be so calculating. I was just as glad the mirror was all fogged up. No use looking myself in the eyes and confessing I'd already calculated a list of the ports of call thirteen thousand dollars would buy. If we stayed on a budget, worked the act from port to port, that thirteen thousand could take Squirl and me halfway around the world!

Maybe I didn't have the courage to turn Babe in myself, but I could sit, watch and do nothing while Squirl turned her in. Justice? Yes. Blood money? Yes, but I couldn't help that.

I went to Squirl's room on the bottom floor. I was kept in luxury, but Squirl had to pay rent for his small room off the kitchen. I'd only been there a few times. Each time to remind him it was time to head over to Luna Park for our shows.

Squirl still slept like a baby, so I had to knock loudly. But he didn't answer. I tried the knob, but it was locked. Strange that on this, of all mornings, when we had so much to talk about, so much to plan, he wasn't there. He should have been camping next to my door, awaiting my answer.

I turned toward the kitchen to get a cup of coffee, when I heard his voice. He was speaking on the kitchen wall phone, leaning against the wall as though he didn't want any of the help to hear. I was going to sneak up on him, slip my arms around his waist and whisper "Yes" into his ear. But I stopped short when I heard him speak into the phone.

"Western Union? I need to send a telegram. This goes to Mrs. Red Hankins, Centner's Mill, Washington. Yes, there's a phone, but you'll have to get the number. No greeting, just these words: 'Ridenour'—that's 'R-I-D-E-N-O-U-R. Stop. Cordelia. Stop. Luna Park. Stop. Urgent. Stop.' Huh? Oh, yeah, close it with 'A concerned friend.' Got that?"

He then told the operator to bill Sally's number.

I backed out of the kitchen and ran across the large entry hall and out into the street. I stopped on the corner and caught my breath.

Oh God, he'd done it! It didn't matter one bloodred cent what my answer was! It wasn't going to take an army at all— all it was going to take was one brief telegram as the lure and me as the bait.

I calmed my ragged breathing, walked back into Cousin Sally's and went up to my room to think. The fact that Squirl had already decided to go ahead without me meant that my calculations had been dead wrong. If two people could get halfway around the world on thirteen thousand dollars, then one person could get all the way around the world. I was betrayed. Plain and simple.

When Babe got the telegram, if she came looking for me it would take her two days to get there, possibly one if she caught a truck coming out of Centner's Mill. I kept telling myself to relax, Babe would simply listen to the telegram, rip the phone off the wall, crush it into powder—then what? That one name, Ridenour, would tell her that she'd been found out. Why would she risk her neck to help me? She'd have to move on and she'd head anywhere but Seattle. She'd leave my father. Unless she really loved him. No, she'd move on. No telling how many husbands she'd left over the years she'd been on the run. What was so bad about that? We'd all get over it.

My eyes came to rest on the telephone in my room. I think I stared at it for an hour. I had to call home. Both Babe and my father knew where I was now, so I had nothing left to hide. It didn't mean I was coming home or giving up or giving in, it just meant I had to call home.

I rehearsed at least fifty different conversations. What would they say to me? I imagined everything from Cordy We Love You Come Home to We Thought You Killed Yourself to Cordy Who? I looked at my hand reaching for the telephone. It was shaking.

I got the operator and gave her the long-distance phone number. She said she'd have to call me back and I knew I'd have to sit by the phone and not risk the chance of anyone but me picking it up.

After fifteen minutes I started to pace. What could be so difficult about connecting a few telephone wires? It wasn't as though I was calling France, for God's sake.

When Squirl opened my door, I nearly jumped.

"Hey, you," he said, coming over to me. "How long have you been up?" He took me in his arms, kissed my head and said, "I haven't even gone to bed yet, thinkin' about us."

"No, I didn't sleep much, either," I said, staring at the phone.

He kept holding me, stroking my hair; then he whispered, "So, what'd you decide? Marry me?"

"Since I first saw you, out on those logs back home, it's

what I've dreamt about," I said. It was true. I did love him. So much.

He kissed me and the phone rang.

"Oh, that's for me," I said, breaking away and going to the phone.

He pulled me back, saying, "Forget it. Someone can take a message."

"No, I . . ."

Squirl smiled down at me, leaned over and picked up the phone. My heart stopped. I watched his face as he said, "Hello?"

His face hardened. He handed me the phone and said, coldly, "The long-distance operator. For you."

He must have known by my face why the long-distance operator was calling me. After all, who else did I have to call?

I took the phone. Squirl held my arm and wouldn't let go.

"Yes?" I said. "Yes . . . I'll wait. . . ." Squirl and I locked eyes and he pulled himself closer to the phone. I listened to the operator. He kissed my face. His breath was warm and silky on my cheek.

"Marry me, Cordy," he whispered in my ear. "Marry me today."

His hand was on the phone and I let him have it. He tossed the phone onto the couch and embraced me totally.

"Come on, say you will," he said.

He more than held me in his embrace, he held me in his trance. I felt weak all over. Then a faraway, familiar and powerful voice said, "Cordy? That you, Cordy?"

Squirl heard it too. The instant our eyes met, we both knew. He leaped for the telephone as I screamed out, "Stay away, Babe!"

We struggled for the phone and I was no match for Squirl's wiry strength, or his anger. He ripped the phone wire out of the wall. He looked at me and said, "You ruined everything, Cordy! You and me could have had it all!" He came over to me, put his hand under my chin and added, "Now we got nothin'!"

"I know about the telegram, Squirl!" I shouted back. "I heard you not an hour ago! You said you'd let *me* call the shots. Let *me* decide about Babe. 'Not unless you're one hundred percent sure, Cordy!' " I repeated for him. "Your exact words, Squirl!"

"We had to act fast!"

"No, *you* had to act fast!"

"Look, Cordy, when I had the Seattle police run down that case—check into the reward and everything—don't you think that opened some eyeballs? Don't you think just maybe a few people, probably even your old friend Chief Daniels, will get a little suspicious? Like hell he wouldn't beat us to Babe—Giganta, that freak—and pocket the reward money himself!"

"No!" I turned my back on him and stared out the window toward the Seattle skyline.

Squirl whirled me around to face him. "Cordy, think! It's only a matter of time before someone turns her in! Why not us? Why shouldn't you be paid for all those years of misery she put you through? For all those binges you pulled her down off of! Remember, Cordy? Remember how much you hated her? How much you hated your father for marryin' her in the first place?"

"That was a whole lifetime ago . . . ," I said weakly.

"Cordy, think! Thirteen thousand dollars! Ours. By the end of the week."

"You'd leave me flat for that money," I said, turning and waiting for his denial.

He again had me by the shoulders. "Is that what you think? Really?" He reached into his pocket and pulled out an envelope. He handed me two tickets for passage to South America on the SS *Albright.* "And I ain't takin' John Wilkes Booth," he said.

"You and me?"

"You and me. Soon as everything's settled. That's what you want, isn't it?"

I sat down and admitted, "Yes, I guess it is."

The key word there was "guess"—"guess," as in confused but not having the guts to admit it.

32

Three days passed. A week. Nothing. Our Indian summer had become early winter. With each passing day, Squirl was growing more agitated and restless. I was growing more re-laxed and calm. If nothing came of Squirl's telegram, maybe I'd have both Squirl and a clear conscience. Although, with each passing day, Squirl stared at me more and more coldly. Or rather, he stared past me, as though he was reading his solution on the walls behind me.

I should have known Squirl wouldn't give up easily. On the seventh day he said to me, "I got another idea. One I should have come up with in the first place." His words were clipped, punctuated, calculated. A different Squirl.

"What?" I asked.

"Gotta hire a few men and go up after her. All's I have to do is register with the Seattle police as a bounty hunter. She's probably taken off by now, so it's the only way."

"Bounty hunter?" I asked, seeing dime Western novels and bodies slung over packhorses and smoking six-shooters and

Billy the Kid. "Come on, Squirl," I said. "That would be risking your life, our future. Why don't we give up on all this reward business. Get on with us?"

"On what, my good looks and your white hair?" he asked back.

"Yes," I answered plainly, "with exactly that. Look, we have the tickets to South America. I have some money saved. . . ."

Squirl looked at me as though I was stupid to even suggest what little money I had could contribute to the lifestyle he'd been planning.

I leaned against the wall and asked right out, "Is it me or the money, Squirl?"

What a stupid question, I told myself even as I was asking it. First of all, I didn't want the truth, and second of all, I knew he'd lie.

"I won't even honor that with an answer," he said, looking out my window toward the gray mist hanging over Puget Sound.

I was wrong. He'd avoided answering it entirely.

"So, it *is* the money," I whispered, mostly to hear myself say it.

There was a brief, helpless look in his eyes. But his expression quickly hardened when he replied, "How come you can't figure out that everything always comes down to money? But don't you burn out a bearing worryin' about *my* problems, Cordy. I can take care of my own problems!"

It was then I realized Squirl couldn't—he couldn't take care of his own problems and he couldn't take care of mine.

I told him I was tired and maybe he'd better leave. He said that was just as well. He had things to do in town, anyway.

And I had things to do too.

It was a chilly parting.

A little while later, Sally knocked on my door. She came in with a tray of hot tea and cookies. Although I'd come to look forward to our girl talk in the evenings when things were slow for her business, I wanted more than anything to be alone that night. I'd been crying and my whole body ached.

She took one look at me and asked, "So, what's wrong?"

"What makes you think something's wrong?"

"Come on, this is Sally," she answered, handing me my tea.

I didn't say anything.

"I'll bet it's that no-good brother of mine, isn't it?"

"No."

"Then what? Aren't you happy here?"

"I love this place, but . . ."

"But what?"

"But maybe I don't belong here," I said.

Sally set her tea down, straightened a little. "I see. Is it because of . . . what goes on here?"

It was funny. In the four months I'd been there, we had really never talked—in exact words—about what "went on" at Cousin Sally's.

I answered no.

"Haven't I always kept you safe? Apart from the back rooms? Treated you like a sister?"

I nodded my head.

She leaned over, touched my hand and said, "Cordelia, the season's over. Do you want to go someplace? Get away?

Maybe see how the ol' folks at home are doing?" She laughed because I'd told her over many a cup of tea just how I felt about "the ol' folks at home."

But I replied, "Yes, you know . . . a change of place might be—"

"I know!" she interrupted. "Let's you and me go to San Francisco! Just drop everything and go! You've never been there and . . ."

So I nodded and smiled and listened to Sally as she told me what fun we'd have, the money we'd just throw away, the parties we'd go to, the sights we'd see, the clothes we'd buy. Even Sally was doing it now—calculating that if we ran away and spent enough money it would solve all our problems. Maybe she and Squirl were more brother and sister than any of us dared to admit. I watched her glide to the fireplace and noticed that she and Squirl had the same confident walk.

I let her go on, but I was preparing for other destinations. I was going to go home. To Centner's Mill. If Babe was still there, I was going to give her the money she would need to leave. If she wasn't, I was going to turn around and head in another direction. Not Seattle. Not San Francisco. Not the South Seas. I'd be gone before my father could even demand to know where I'd been and what I'd been doing to earn so much money. I had a whole trunk full of costumes and a scrapbook of my wondrous abilities onstage. I'd show him those, then leave. I would send for my sweet friend—maybe my *only* friend—Halbie. I'd be safe with him. He knew shows elsewhere and could set us up.

No more Squirl.

Clean conscience, clean slate, clean start.

This had all been a fairy-tale life in a place where nothing was real. A huge Ten in One show. This place, Luna Park, even Sally. It had been fun while it lasted, but now winter was coming on and Cinderella's foot no longer fit the slipper.

Sally finally left, and I wondered if I was going to miss her. She was going to miss me, I knew that. Odd creature that I was, I think I was the only *normal* person she knew. I went to my closet to sort out what was mine and what was borrowed from Sally. This break was going to be clean.

I heard a noise, a *ping*, like a pebble on glass. I came out of my closet and looked down on the street. I turned off a lamp to cut the glare and looked again.

Halbie was in the street. He was dressed as a man—a first for me, and I almost didn't recognize him. I opened the window and leaned out.

"Cordy!" he called up.

"That you, Halbie?" I called back down. "Come on up."

"I can't. I have to catch the ten-fifteen."

"Where you going?"

"Away. The South, the East, I don't know. Anywhere but the West!"

"Why? What's wrong?"

"That Squirl of yours is going to get us all killed!"

"Halbie," I called, leaning as far out the window as I dared. "Why? What's wrong?"

"Giganta's in town, that's what. I don't want nothing to do with it! No blood money, no ticket to the South Seas, no nothing! No one said nothing about violence!"

I wasn't sure I was hearing right. I looked down at Halbie, almost dumb. "Babe's *here*?" I asked. "Here in Luna Park?"

"Yes, Cordy! She—"

I moved back inside and leaned against the window.

Think! I had to think! So she'd come for me. Who knew her reasons? It didn't matter, I guess. Babe had come for *me!*

"Cordy?" Halbie cried up again.

I called back down, "Wait, Halbie! Wait there!"

Halbie looked around nervously. I put on my coat, pulled on my boots and climbed down the fire escape. Halbie helped me down the last half story.

"There's nothing you or me can do, Cordy," he said anxiously. "Squirl's a wild man. Crazy. I've seen him get crazy before, but never like this."

"I need your help, Halbie."

"Honey, I'm just a second-rate sideshow freak, not some storybook hero. Let me go, Cordy. Please. There's going to be bloodshed. You come with me. Forget that Squirl. Boy like him'll end up dead soon anyhow."

"You go, Halbie," I said. "But tell me where Babe is. Maybe I can . . ."

"She was seen camping on that hill up there. We were having a bowl of chowder at the café and this man came in, white as a ghost. Said he'd run across this huge giant up in the hills, camping out. Said it near scared him to death. It's her, Cordy. You just know it has to be."

"Does Squirl know?" I asked.

"He was sitting right next to me. He told me to call the Seattle police. Then he took off. Oh, Cordy, I did. I did call them. What was I to do? I was thinking about our plans to run away and all. Cordy, let it all alone. I have to go. You know how it is."

Halbie apologized for his cowardice, kissed me on the cheek and sped off toward the ferry terminal.

I watched him disappear into the chilly fog. Then I began walking toward Luna Park.

33

I was thinking as I walked how strange it was: Just last week I was taking curtain calls as Cordelia, Daughter of the Orient, and practicing saying my married name. And now I was risking everything I'd become, everything I had, to save Babe. Babe . . . Giganta . . . the very person who, in a way, had forced me to Seattle to begin with.

Babe was camping up there, somewhere. But where? We were surrounded by woods. Although many people camped in Schmitz Park and even on the beach, Babe would hide deep in the woods and stay there, planning her next move.

Where could I get a truck? I wondered. If I could hire a truck, convince Babe she had to stay hidden and then get her out of town—"convince Babe," did I say? Now, there were two words that never belonged together. Besides, a truck out of town was too easy to track down, overtake. I looked out over the lights on the water. The water. A boat. Hire a boat, get Babe out of town using the vastness of the foggy Puget Sound. Perfect.

I knew I'd need money—lots of it. I would be buying not only the services of the boat and its captain, I would also be buying his silence. I knew I had almost five hundred dollars hidden in my closet. I could probably get Babe as far as Vancouver, Canada, on that money. Thoughts of aiding and abetting a murderess did not even enter into it. We'd solve that one later. Only two things were certain: She'd come to help *me*, and Squirl wasn't going to get one cent off of her.

I knew I had to be cunning and calculating from that point on. More so than Squirl. I needed to go back to Sally's, get my money, pack a few things, then secure a boat. Then find Babe.

I got as far as the corner. An arm whirled me around and I was pulled into the dark alley.

"Cordelia!" a man whispered, his face in the shadows.

"I thought you—" I said.

"Now, just listen: I'm scared to death and God knows I couldn't care less about proving my manhood," Halbie said. "But I can't leave you now."

His face hardened, his lips tightened as though he was conquering a demon or fighting to keep emotions inside. He added carefully, "For once. For once I'm staying to fight."

I smiled, but before I could speak, he added, "Squirl has a gun and two thugs he picked up off the wharf. I know that blood look in a man's eye, Cordy. I saw a lynch mob go after a shoeblack once in Selma. I know that look. I hoped I'd never see it again."

"Look, Halbie, I have a plan. I need you to go to the wharf and hire a boat. Something big enough—you know, cabins and everything. One with a motor, if you can. Not a sailboat. I'm going to get money. Cost doesn't matter, just get the boat."

"Okay," Halbie said. "Then what?"

"Stay with the boat. I'm better in the woods than Squirl. I'll find Babe before he does, get her to follow me. God, if we can just keep the police out of this . . ."

Halbie turned.

"Halbie!" I said, grabbing his arm. "The police. What did they say when you called them?"

"They said they'd look into it. I don't think they took me too seriously, once I told them who I was."

I looked out over the waterfront. There were no precincts back then in West Seattle, so I knew, if they did take Halbie's call seriously, it would take them a while to get over here.

"Oh, Cordy, people are going to die and it'll be all my fault!"

"Not if I can help it, Halbie," I said.

We went back to Sally's and he helped me up the fire escape and then vanished into the darkness. I only hoped he could hold himself together long enough to do his part. I quickly gathered my belongings, then went to my closet to get my money.

I should have known better. There was all of forty-two dollars and some change left. I almost laughed at my trusting stupidity. What about my other hiding place in my shoe box? Empty. Squirl hadn't missed a trick.

I was going to turn fifteen next month. I don't know why that thought occurred to me just then, except perhaps I was thinking a fifteen-year-old would have known better. It was time I took off my smoked glasses, kept them off and saw things for what they were.

No money, no boat, no escape.

And so a thief was born. I took the jewelry Sally had

entrusted to me and wondered if she would feel about me the way I was now feeling about her brother.

But unlike Squirl, I left an IOU and my plea for forgiveness in the jewelry box.

Sally,
   I'm so sorry. I have my reasons. You've been my sister, mother, confessor, nurse. I promise, I'll pay you back.
Cordy

That was the best I could do.

I went back out into the night, the same way I'd left earlier. Without Halbie down on the street to help me, I had to drop from the fire escape and was just lucky I didn't snap an ankle or, worse yet, have someone see me.

It must have been around midnight and I was thankful the moon was hidden. I made sure my hair was safely tucked into my cap, for its whiteness could betray me as I passed under a streetlight.

The woods now. Where to begin? Halbie had pointed to the hills overlooking Luna Park. I looked up. The fog was thick, hiding us all. I knew of a trail the kids took as a shortcut into the park and decided that was where I'd go. If Squirl knew of that trail, I was following him.

The advantage of fog is the way it somehow holds sounds in, as though to say, you may not be able to see through me, but you can hear better than ever. So I stopped to listen. I only heard the lapping of water from the shore below and the gentle chug of a steam engine. The ferry must have just come in. I walked to the hillside, straining to catch a glimpse of the passengers as they walked off. I could hear laughing, someone coughing, but nothing that told me if any of the passengers were policemen from Seattle.

Stop wondering and just search all the faster, I warned myself. I began to climb the trail. I found my stride and remembered how, in the hills back home, I could almost run up hillsides, like a mountain goat, fearless.

I kept stopping to listen, and to search the darkness for a lantern or a campfire. I couldn't hear anything. Good, I told myself.

I crested the hill and was relieved to see the fog was hugging Puget Sound below, leaving the hillside clear. I looked up and saw stars. From here I could see a scrub meadow where some early loggers had clear-cut. And beyond the clearing, I could barely make out a wispy spiral of smoke. I took a deep breath. Yes! A campfire. Babe?

I hiked up my skirts and ran across the clearing, running around huge log stumps and slash piles, trusting God with every leap that maybe I *could* see better in the dark.

I stopped just short of the campsite and caught my breath.

I ventured closer to make sure. All forests lure men who need to be hidden—that was the first rule. It would be just my luck to walk smack-dab into a den of thieves. As I carefully inched closer, I could feel my pockets sag with the weight of Sally's jewelry and thought maybe I'd be right at home with a gang of thieves.

I didn't have to look beyond the shadows the embers cast to see the hulk of Babe, sitting on a log, gnawing on a loaf of crusty bread.

Before I could call out her name, she knew I was there. Her head came up like a she-bear looking around, searching for her cubs. I'd often thought that Babe was sometimes more animal than human. If she was sniffing the wind for the intruder's scent, I wouldn't have been surprised.

"Babe?" I whispered. "It's me. Cordy."

She stood up, dropped the bread loaf, turned around.

"Who's there?" she demanded.

I came in closer. "Me, Babe. Cordy."

I entered the golden arc of the firelight and stood, thinking she'd do one of three things: run to kill me, run to hug me or sit back down and finish her loaf of bread.

She looked at me, almost smiled and said, "Didn't think you'd kill yourself. You're braver'n that. Your pa thought maybe you would, but I never once believed it. When the mill struck, I thought your pa'd go crazy. Like as how everyone turned on him. I left too. I been out lookin' for you. Aberdeen. Longview. Ilwaco. Been all over the place. Finally went home to check on yer pa. That's when that telegram come through. Yer pa cried, Cordy. Broke down and cried like a baby."

She picked up the bread, whacked some pine needles off of it and offered it to me. "You et lately?"

"Babe, I've come to warn you. It's not safe here."

Babe smiled and I noticed she'd lost another tooth. "I got me some Campbell's soup in the tent. Tomato, I think. You always liked tomato. You want some soup?"

"Babe," I continued, taking the bread from her. "Come on, we don't have much time." I started to fold her bedroll.

But Babe just sat down on the log, took a stick, stirred the fire up and looked at me through the pops and crackles of the rising embers.

"You couldn'ta come to a worser place, Cordy," she said.

Her mighty jaw flexed and yet her eyes were almost serene through the blurring smoke.

"Quit stirring that fire, they'll find us," I said, taking the stick from her.

She just stared at me. How many times had she done that? Over the dirty pots in the kitchen, across the Sunday dinner table, from her huge rocking chair on the porch.

Her face was somehow less grotesque in the firelight, almost kind. She reached into her coat pocket and pulled out one of the flyers on me, held it up and said, "Found this in Olympia. You've let him make you a freak, Cordy. Ridenour and his circus of sorry, wore-out—what's he call 'em— nondescripts? I would have moved that damn mountain back home to have kept you from this."

"Babe, we have to go. I have a boat waiting. Come on," I said, ignoring her and kicking dirt into the fire.

She watched me for a few minutes; then, just as the fire was smoldering and the smoke was thick between us, she whispered, "I didn't kill no one, Cordy."

I had never, never in all the years I'd known Babe, heard her whisper. I sat down and watched her face. I saw the slight reflection of tears in her large black eyes.

"I know you didn't," I whispered back. It just came out. I had been perfectly willing to believe Babe had the ability to kill half of Seattle if she wanted to, but hearing her voice, seeing her tear-filled eyes, I knew she hadn't.

"Had me a little friend, little Carlotta. Emil Ridenour was always extra mean to her. I kept steppin' in. Then one night, Eben—we was married—comes in and sees Emil and me arguin'. He loved me, Eben did. Folks thought he was bad as Emil, exploitin' the likes of me and Carlotta. Anyhow, the four of us had it out. Had us a big fight. Words turned ugly. Maybe we'd been drinkin', I don't remember. Emil pulled a gun on me. Guns don't scare me none and I took it from him. Eben stepped in and Ridenour killed him—my Eben. Hit him with a crowbar. Looked like something I might have done," she said, keeping her eyes on my face. Then she added almost sheepishly, "Like you know, I got me a temper. Back then I was even worst. But Cordy, I didn't kill no one—but me—when I ran."

"You don't have to tell me anyth—" I began, but she cut me off.

"I come to finish what I started all them years ago in Chicago. Ridenour turned me into a freak, killed my husband and said I done it. Even puts up a reward to keep me hid. Ridenour ruint my whole life, Cordy. Now he's doing it to you. I come to kill him, Cordy. Ain't no more running away for me. In for a dime, in for a dollar, I always say."

"Babe, it doesn't have to be this way. I have a boat. Canada is just a day's ride north."

"Then what?"

Her voice was almost small, almost helpless, and I understood her as well as if I'd uttered that question myself. Yes, then what? More running.

"I have money. We'll get you a lawyer, reopen the case, bring Ridenour to justice, Babe," I said.

Babe just smiled and repeated the word "justice" a few times over—as though she'd never heard it before and liked the way the "j" and the "c" danced upon her tongue.

She finally looked over to me and whispered, "Okay, Cordy. Okay. Justice."

34

We pulled together what few things Babe had brought with her, leaving the tent standing. I led the way back through the clearing. But, unlike me, creeping was not Babe's style. She snapped low branches off rather than stoop under them, kicked and swore at logs that tripped her, and took big heavy steps that surely most of West Seattle could hear, maybe even feel under them.

I finally stopped, looked up at her and said, "What we're trying to do here, Babe, is *sneak* down to the waterfront."

"I never snuck nowhere in my whole life and I ain't gonna start now. I may have run, but I never once was quiet about it," she growled down at me. The old Babe, as I had always known her, was back.

By the time we had worked our way to the trail down to Luna Park, the fog was beginning to lift over the Sound. I was hoping it would have thickened, but a breeze was coming off the Sound and I knew, between Babe's feelings about sneaking and now no cloak of fog, we would have to be very clever.

Several times I made her stop and sit down while I went further down the trail to see how things might be developing on the waterfront below.

I could now hear voices, which made me stop cold. It was maybe two or three in the morning by then—no one should have been down there at all. I ventured farther down and hid among some low fir branches. I had to squint hard, but I could make out the helmets of the Seattle police.

Oh God, I thought, please help Halbie be strong. I envisioned him breaking in two as the police grilled him on what he was doing there. Please give him the courage to lie.

I knew it was suicide to try to stay by the waterfront. So I led us in the direction of Luna Park, where there were places to hide, to wait, to watch.

Thank God I'd walked these streets alone late at night, thank God I'd been so comfortable in the dark. I pulled Babe along, taking her by the hand when she said she couldn't see a blasted thing, leading her around trash cans, crates and two terrified raccoons.

Knowing Squirl was out there, armed, flanked with two other men, made turning each new corner more frightening than the last. We were finally within sprinting distance of the gate.

Luna Park, closed up and sealed for the winter, had only a few lights for the occasional passing of the watchman. The path that led to the museum was lit, and I wondered if taking Babe inside the park would be too risky. After all, Ridenour could be anywhere. Maybe gambling at Sally's, or maybe sleeping in his room above the museum.

I thought of the boarded-up arcade and the rows of small anterooms behind each amusement. Easy to get into and far away from the lit path. I had been granted a key to the front gates months ago and used it. Whereas I could nearly squeeze through the opening, I had to get Babe through. The gates creaked as I eased them open and the leaves rustled at our feet. It's amazing the sounds little things can make when you beg for silence.

"Over here, Babe," I whispered, pulling her along through the shadows of the boarded-up midway.

She stopped and looked around at the skeleton of the roller coaster, the giant whirl-o-swing now silent, the Ferris wheel without riders, a lonely gathering of huge spokes against the horizon.

"Babe, hurry," I urged.

"I'll bet I played a million joints like this," she said, her eyes falling on the banner that announced Dr. Ridenour's Carnival of Mystic Delights. She pointed to it and said, "He ain't even sprung for a new banner. Tight as McKenzie's nuts, he is."

"Babe, now!" I said, using the tone she'd so often used on me.

She glowered down at me but came anyway.

I found a room behind the ringtoss. The couple who ran it were elderly and I knew they'd outfitted their back room with two beds, which I pulled together to make one large one for Babe.

I made sure the window was sealed before risking screwing in the lightbulb swinging over my head. The room came to eerie life, with the painted faces of Kewpie dolls smiling down at us, wrapped in cellophane and awaiting next year's rubes. Chubby dolls, stuffed donkeys and rubber animal squeak toys sat at attention on the shelves.

"You hungry?" I asked Babe, remembering the half-eaten loaf of bread in her pack.

She looked at me as though that was the stupidest question of all time. Babe was always hungry. "Look, why don't you lie down, get some rest? I'm going to find our boat out of here."

"What about justice?" she asked me, with as close to a wry smile as I'd ever seen on her. "I told you I wasn't running no more."

"Babe, we have to get away from here. We'll set you up on one of the islands. Far away. Then I'll hire an attorney. I know it sounds stupid, but I have connections here in Seattle. I promise you. But for now, you're not safe here."

She very carefully sat down on the bed, testing its strength first, then easing her entire weight down. She took one of the Kewpie dolls down, ripped the cellophane off and made it squeak.

"I could use something hot. My insides is all cold."

"I know a place that opens for the fishermen in about an hour. I'll go make our connection, then bring you back something. Coffee, maybe some soup."

"Soup'd be good," she said, still staring down at the coy little smile on the doll.

I tried to unscrew the lightbulb but found looking up at it was hard on my eyes. I reached for it. Babe stood up, slapped my hand away from the hot bulb and twisted it off.

"I keep tellin' you, girl, you'll ruin your eyes."

"I'll be back in an hour. Don't get worried if it's longer. I need to be careful," I whispered in the dark.

"I ain't never once worried about you, Cordy," Babe said flatly, laying her great frame down on the groaning springs.

I knew now that wasn't true. Babe *had* worried about me, and more than once.

35

If stealing into Luna Park to hide Babe was easy for me, working my way along the well-lit waterfront to the wharf wasn't. My white face reflected even the smallest speck of light, and there was far too much activity for my liking. I did what I could. I reached into the sandy loam in the planter boxes and rubbed dirt on my face.

I looked down the two docks that comprised the wharf and strained to see any light. I wished to hell I'd thought of wearing my dungarees. My skirts would be all too obvious to anyone who might spy a smallish person running along the waterfront. A runaway boy might not cause much suspicion—but something in skirts . . .

Then I saw a man sitting on a bench overlooking the ferry landing. I came a little closer to make sure. Yes, it was!

I tossed a pebble into the water in front of him. He jerked around. Poor Halbie, I'm sure he was aging years by the hour that night.

"Halbie?" I whispered.

"Cordy?" he whispered back. "Oh my God, they're looking everywhere," he said. "Didn't you see them? Cops, five of them!"

"Where?" I asked.

"I saw you and Giganta come down off the trail so I told the cops I heard something down that way." He pointed in the opposite direction. "Cordy, did you fall? Your face . . ."

"Where's Squirl?" I asked.

"He sent his men that way," he said, pointing west. "Then he took off toward the hillside." Halbie looked a little proud of himself when he added, "I told him someone had seen the giant head west. I lied. I lied to the cops and I lied to Squirl."

I hugged him and he showed me the boat he'd secured for us. I dug into my pockets and handed Halbie Sally's jewels. "Here. For the captain."

"All of this?"

"No. You know the value of this stuff more than me. You're in charge."

Our plan was set. I would go and get Babe, bring her back just as the predawn darkness was blackest and Squirl and the police were looking in other directions. Then we'd be off.

I made my way back to Luna Park and slipped in the gates without any trouble. I was oddly proud of Halbie for standing up to the authorities and lying so well. I know he lied all the time when he, as Countess Polanski, told fortunes to paying customers, but lying into a policeman's eyes or, harder still, Squirl's . . . Good work, Halbie.

I remembered how hard it was to shake Babe awake sometimes, so I didn't think twice about her not coming to the door when I lightly knocked. I turned the knob and was angry, after all my night's work, that she hadn't bothered to lock it.

"Babe, you . . ."

I knew, without turning on the light, that Babe wasn't there. I ran out into the back alley and listened. Knowing Babe, I would be hearing something—a bench, a trash can—being knocked over before long.

It didn't even occur to me that she would go looking for Ridenour, until I heard a high-pitched scream coming from the museum.

I ran up the path, through the maze of picnic tables and over a hedge. I scrambled up the steps and saw the front door to the museum open, the glass broken. Another scream, coming from downstairs. I ran toward the back hallway and saw a dancing light coming from the stairwell. I sailed down the stairs.

"Oh God, Babe, no . . . ," I said as I entered the laboratory.

Babe was holding a large tree limb high in the air. "This is perfecter than I ever dreamed of," Babe said.

Ridenour and Carlotta were standing up against the wall.

"Babe," I said, "put it down."

Instead, she took a step closer and raised her weapon even higher, ready to strike.

"I oughta kill you, too, Carlotta, bein' as how it was you who started the whole thing," Babe growled.

"Fern . . . ," Carlotta said, her face not terrified, not angry, but filled with pleading. "Please . . . I tried to find you . . . to tell you . . ."

"Stop talking, Carlotta. I crossed the line once to keep *him* from you. Finding you here with him means I did it for nothin'!"

"No, that's not—"

But Babe raised her arm higher and screamed, "No!" After the word stopped echoing about the room, she closed her eyes and seemed to struggle for control. "Carlotta, you was once my only friend. I don't kill friends—even them that turncoats on me! So you git!"

Carlotta hesitated, and Babe looked as though she was going to crush the dwarf. Carlotta screamed, "I'm sorry I'm sorry I'm sorry!" as she ran down the back hallway.

Babe inched closer to Ridenour. "You look at my Cordy here and tell her I don't got good reason to kill you."

"Your Cordy?" Ridenour asked. "What does that little white freak have to do with you?"

Babe's face dissolved in rage. She whirled the limb around her and smashed everything in its path. A section of a lab table fell over, vials spilled and gasses erupted. Babe walked through the lab, overturning everything. She grabbed jars, chairs, equipment—anything—and threw it at Ridenour, screaming and swearing as she did. He fell and frantically tried to get back up as debris rained down on him.

I followed Babe, pulling at her dress, using all my might to try to bring her to her senses. I screamed and she shook me off the way you shake a kitten off your skirts.

Ridenour finally stood up and looked Babe directly in the eyes. "I should have killed you when I had a chance!"

Babe put down the chair she was holding over her head. She simply motioned him to come closer and said, "You wan' another chance? Come on, Emil. Take me on."

His face hardened and he quickly looked around the floor for a weapon. His eyes landed on a pair of long shears. He seized them and held them in front of him while he slowly came toward Babe. "Someone should have drowned you the day you were born," he growled.

Babe just looked at him. He lunged, she grabbed the shears and it wasn't really a struggle at all. She twisted them out of his hands as though she was taking a pencil from a child. Then she backhanded him, sending him reeling back down into the pile of overturned furniture.

I screamed again for her to stop but she kept tearing apart the room like an elephant gone mad.

The last thing Babe found to hurl was an oil lamp.

"Babe, stop!" I shrieked, trying to catch her arm as she swung it back. I almost went through the air with the lantern. I could smell the oil as it splashed down on the heap of objects.

She looked around for a match.

"No, Babe! That's enough! No more!"

She paused a moment, almost as if she heard me and came back to her senses. Then she reached into her pocket and brought out a match. She lit it with her thumbnail and said, "You keep your justice and I'll keep mine." Then she tossed the match onto the oozing oil on the floor.

Ridenour screamed as the flames quickly grew. The room filled with smoke and suddenly it was a mass of flames and confusion. Babe reached out in the smoke and grabbed me. She scooped me into her arms like so much kindling and headed for the hall. The door, half off its hinges, had stuck in the doorjamb and for a moment I thought we couldn't get out.

Babe set me down, grabbed the door's edge and gave a mighty tug and it simply snapped all the way off its hinges. She hurled it across the room like it was as light as balsa.

Babe scooped me up again and carried me out of the blazing room.

She stopped only when she'd carried me outside and safely away. She put me down. I don't know what I was screaming, thinking, even doing. I could feel the warmth of the burning building on my face. Carlotta must have sounded the fire alarm, because men were shouting and running around with fire hoses. I screamed to a passing fireman that someone— Emil Ridenour—was still downstairs.

In the smoky shadows I saw two men bringing Ridenour out. They laid him on the ground and I came closer. He was writhing and coughing, but he was alive. Babe was not a murderess, after all.

I stood a few moments longer, watching in disbelief as the medical museum and its cabinet of nondescripts began to burn—all those hapless "wonders," consumed at last.

I turned around, searching the crowd. Babe was gone.

36

I looked frantically around for Babe. The sky was now lit with the fire's glow. The natatorium was the closest building to me, so that was the first place I ran to. At the entrance I realized I'd chosen right, for the glazed glass on the doors was shattered.

I went inside. I'd only been there one other time, but not to swim, of course. I knew you could get to the pool through the dressing rooms. I ran through, calling for Babe as I went.

The building was nearly all glass, adding to its humid warmth all year round. I could tell by the filtered emerald light that the sun was beginning to rise. The horribly growing fire lit the natatorium from the south.

The huge pool was surrounded by French doors, which opened up to the larger outside pool on Puget Sound for the summer bathers. If Babe had made her way that far, she'd have gone as far as she could go, with nothing but the chilly waters of Puget Sound for her refuge.

"Babe!" I screamed, my voice resounding off the walls and the water in the pool. Wavy glints of water reflected upon the glass walls. There, across the giant room, pacing like a cornered lioness, was Babe.

"You go away, Cordy! I ain't sorry I done that! You told me 'justice.' Well, don't you know there's only one kind of justice for Ridenour? Don't you know there's only one kind of justice for *me*?"

"Babe!" I called. "Let me help you! Quick!"

"*Noooooo!*" she screamed. "You git out of here!"

I tried to calm Babe, to tell her that Ridenour wasn't dead, that we could still bring him to justice.

But Babe climbed into the bleachers and shouted, "No! Cordy, no! You go home! Hide in them trees! Yer safe in them trees!"

Then I heard a noise behind me. I turned and was blinded by a lantern in my face.

"Good on you, Cordy. You got her cornered," Squirl said, lowering the lamp.

It took a moment to get my vision back. "Squirl, it's off! Leave her be!"

He set the lantern down while he said smoothly, "Your big mistake was tellin' that fireman Ridenour was down in that fire. You should have kept your mouth shut and let him burn up. I was right there. Watched the whole thing from the shadows."

"That wasn't my big mistake, Squirl . . . my big mistake was—"

He cut me off. It was as though he didn't hear me.

" 'Cause if Ridenour was dead, then gettin' to that reward might have been a little tricky. Reckon now he'll want her dead more'n ever. Maybe even give me a bonus. So in a way, you, my dear, just put the last nail in her coffin. As you can see, the deal is still on."

He pulled out a gun.

"No, Squirl!"

"Look at her," he said, pointing to Babe, who was now climbing back down the bleachers. "She ain't nothin' more'n a killer animal."

She lumbered down an aisle until she was nearly above Squirl's head.

"What're you gonna do?" he asked up at her, laughing and holding his gun on her. "Squash me flat?"

"I'm begging you, Squirl," I whispered, pulling his arm. "If I ever meant anything to you!"

"Well, you did . . . once." He turned on me and put the gun to my forehead. "I really need that money, Cordy. Nothing's stopping me. Not even you."

He would do it, I thought. I know he would.

Babe knew it too.

She screamed—not a human scream and like nothing I'd heard ever before.

Squirl whirled toward her and shot as she scrambled down from the bleachers. He hit her in the arm, but she still lumbered forward and then backhanded Squirl with her good arm.

He sailed into the water as though he'd dived in, and she followed after him.

I watched, helpless, as they struggled underwater. Babe held him down. He came up, gasping for air, struggling for his life. Then she pulled him down again—longer.

"Stop it! Stop it!" I screamed.

I heard the muted sound of the gun going off, and the

238

water immediately began to redden. The surface of the water calmed. Finally Babe came up with a huge gasp for air and threw Squirl's limp and bleeding body up and across the pool.

She stood in the water, breathing heavily, looking around confused. Then our eyes met. It was as though she finally realized that the floating body was Squirl. *My* Squirl. She looked at his body across the pool.

We heard the piercing sound of a police whistle outside and Babe seemed to panic. She said, "I ain't sorry, Cordy! Not for nothing! He woulda killed us both, a boy like him!"

Then the doors crashed open and two policemen rushed to the pool and aimed their guns down at her.

"Out of the water!" one commanded.

"She'll come out. Just don't shoot," I said. I know tears were distorting my vision—my vision of Squirl's body, floating facedown in the pool, and of Babe, the water to her chest, looking around, face panicked.

"Babe, come on out slow," I pleaded. "They won't hurt you."

"It's just a matter of how many I can take with me. In for a dime . . . ," she said, looking at each officer's gun.

"Come on, lady," one officer said, walking slowly toward the pool steps. "Come this way."

Two other officers had come in through the locker room doors and had pulled Squirl's body out of the water.

"Look out, Phinney. He's been shot. She might still have the gun!" the officer said.

"It was his gun!" I yelled to them. "It was an accident. They were struggling!"

Another officer called out, "I see the gun! There, at the bottom."

Babe started to ford her way toward me.

"No, over this way!" an officer called out. "To the steps!"

Babe ignored him, looked up at me and asked, " 'Member the last time you saw me in the water?"

It was the swimming lesson in the millpond back home. "Course I remember," I said. "You threw me into the pond. But I got even." I kneeled down on the pool deck and reached my hand out to her, like sweet-talking a child to come in for her nap.

I noticed her lips were turning blue and she was starting to shake, sending little tidal waves scattering out.

"I knew you'd turn out okay from that day on," she said, giving me an oddly warm smile over her chattering teeth.

"Come on out, Babe. Like he says. Swim over there," I pleaded.

Babe looked up at me, shrugged her mighty shoulders and said, "That's the damn funny part of it, Cordy. I don't know how to swim. Looks like I ain't never gonna learn."

With that, she pulled herself out of the water and began walking toward the nearest officer.

"Stop right there," he warned, pulling back the hammer on his gun. "Please, lady. Stop!"

She kept going. He shot low. She paused, looking down at her leg, which was starting to bleed.

I ran to her and faced her square on. I looked up at her and commanded, "You stop now, Babe! You ain't thinkin' of no one but yourself!"

"Out of the way, miss!" the officer warned.

Babe looked down at me, then over my head at the officer and his gun aimed at us both, then around the pool where the other officers had their guns trained on us.

"You going to make them go through me to get to you?" I asked her.

She seemed to be thinking. The only sound was the gentle lapping of the water.

Babe then looked me in the eyes and calmly said, "Yer pa'd kill me if I let anything happen to you."

The guns slowly came down and Babe surrendered.

We wrapped her two gunshot wounds with towels. Babe just sat and let herself be tended to—like all those times when she was on a toot—only now she was cold sober and I was glad to help.

They put Squirl's body on a stretcher, covered him with some towels and carried him over to me.

One of the officers asked, "You know this boy, miss?" They lifted a towel and I looked at his face. Even in death, his face seemed full of promise and mischief.

"Yes," I whispered.

"You'll have to come with us to make a statement," he said, placing the towel back over Squirl's face. I nodded and turned back to Babe.

"You loved that Squirl, didn't you, Cordy?" Babe asked as they carried Squirl away.

I tied a knot in Babe's leg bandage and knew there was nothing I could do to hide my tears.

"I probably would have jumped off a bridge for him," I said. "Yesterday."

The four policemen came over to take Babe back to the jail hospital in Seattle. I followed behind.

I'll always have the memory of Babe, lumbering along in spite of her wounds, two armed policemen in front and two in back, as they disappeared into the smoky mist that hung low over Luna Park that morning.

37

It was an odd hand dealt to me that day. I'd never in my whole life been dealt what Squirl used to call a "surefire hand," where all the cards line up, kings, queens and jacks, and all smile and say, "Bet it all, kid."

In a way, I had bet it all.

The murder trial is set for January fifth in Chicago. But it's not the trial you might think. It will be Emil Ridenour on trial. During the investigation, Carlotta came forward, went to Chicago and gave a deposition to the Cook County District Attorney, telling everything she remembered about that long-ago Chicago murder. She's still there, awaiting the trial. I wonder if she and Babe will ever be friends again.

Babe wasn't charged in either the arson or in Squirl's death. My statement clearly pointed toward self-defense in both cases. And if the lock of my lucky white hair in Chief of Police Daniels's watch helped any, then so be it.

It's a cold day at the King Street Station here in Seattle.

Today is January 2, 1919. Babe has just left for Chicago. She promised to come back the minute she's done watching Ridenour squirm after all the years he'd made her squirm. But she said she belongs to the Northwest now, to Centner's Mill.

" 'Sides," she added, smiling as she boarded the train, "that's where I got me my coffin. If yer ol' man ain't turned it to kindling out of spite, that is. Maybe you oughta go see if yer ol' Babe's still got her coffin, Cordy."

"Maybe I oughta."

She leaned way down and we carefully hugged goodbye. It was our first-ever embrace. I handed her up her valise and said, "Packed you a dozen cans of soup. Tomato."

Then I watched her stuff her bulky frame up the steps and into the train. I stood back watching the astonished faces of the other passengers as Babe lumbered her way down the aisle, hunched over, knocking people with her valise, looking for a set of seats to occupy.

The train pulled out and once again, I was alone in Seattle.

So yes. I'll go back home, to Centner's Mill. When Babe finally called my father after the fire and explained things, he asked to speak to me, but I left the hotel room, not wanting to speak to him. Babe told me he was running the mill with just some scab labor, that he would have come if he could have. I thought he would have come if he'd wanted to, strike or no strike.

Then the oddest thing happened. On December twenty-eighth, my fifteenth birthday, he called me. He asked me to come home after Babe left for Chicago. He said, "I want you to think about coming home. All's I'm doing is asking you to think about it. Oh, and Cordy? Happy birthday."

It was a short conversation, but, in a way, one of our best. It won't be easy going back to Centner's Mill. There's a lot my father and I don't know about each other. Maybe it's time, now that I'm fifteen, that we try to find those things out. Who knows? We might even be friends someday. But I have a feeling it will always be like pushing a boulder uphill, my father and me. I don't know, I guess as long as we keep pushing, all things are possible. Just look at all the things that have happened to me since that June day when I first saw Squirl.

Squirl—even saying his name cues a kiss. My magical, deadly Squirl. You know, it's odd. Of all the journeys I may ever take in this life, they all will have begun with Squirl. So, no, I don't hate him. How can you hate someone who has taught you how to love? Or how *not* to love? I could never really hate Squirl.

I wonder if it's true what they say about your first love—that you never, ever really forget it. That those small "first things"—like a crooked grin or an I-dare-you glance—you will look for on the faces of all future loves. I hope it's true. I really do, for if it is, then in a way, I will always have a little something of Squirl to love.

No matter what, my life is just now taking off—like me in those widow's weeds flying over Puget Sound on July 3, 1918. I intend on finding out someday the other places and hearts I can fly to. There is no turning back now for Cordelia—Daughter of the Orient, and stepdaughter of Babe. All things are possible for a girl the likes of me.

ABOUT THE AUTHOR

RANDALL BETH PLATT lives in the Puget Sound area of Washington State, where she shares her life with her husband, two sons, and assorted creatures large and small. When not at home writing, she can be found on the YMCA handball courts training for a tournament. If she's not in either of those two places, she's on the Oregon coast, where the words seem to come easier. This is her second novel for Delacorte Press.